Alpha Grayson

Midika Crane

This book is published by Inkitt – Join now to read and discover free upcoming bestsellers!

Prologue

My assistant turns from where he was facing the board and looks at me with confusion. He's not really my assistant. In fact, he hates it when I refer to him as that, but I wouldn't go as far to say that this man, Adrian, is my friend.

"Cross him off the list." I request.

"Why?" He asks as he balances a red permanent marker between his fingers. Rolling my eyes, I back up a few steps and sit on the edge of my desk. I try to be mindful of the papers scattered across it.

"You think the Alpha of Love is my mate?" I ask while trying to hide my laughter.

He tilts his head. "Possibly."

I kick my feet together as I stare up at the board mounted on the wall. We are in my office, trying to narrow down who my mate could be. I know he's an Alpha, which gives me 12 options. Unless the Moon Goddess decided to play a personal joke, and pair me with the female Alpha of Independence.

"You're being ridiculous. Picture me with Malik!" I shiver at the thought as I look at his name on the board.

I've met Malik before, although only briefly. When I walked into that room and our eyes met, there was nothing there. At one point, our shoulders touched and no sparks erupted. He's not my mate.

"Are you even sure your mate is an Alpha?" Adrian asks again as he draws a straight red line through Malik's name.

"Yes, our current Luna told me herself and she was once a Purity Pack member. Those freaks don't lie," I tell him. He shrugs, placing the lid of the pen back on.

Adrian scrunches his face up. He wasn't always stuck here in the Vengeance Pack like me. While he was originally from the Wisdom Pack, I was from the Discipline Pack. Neither of us want to go back to our old Packs. We belong here now, completely bound to the Vengeance Pack. Even if the only reason I am here is because I was kidnapped at the age of 13.

Now that I'm older, I have become a leader. Kaden, the Alpha of Vengeance, allowed me a small portion of his land after I released his brother and told him where his parents were. I didn't mean to put my fingers into something that wasn't my business, but I couldn't help myself.

"Cross off Kaden and Landon while you're at it. Both are mated," I request and Adrian obliges. I stare at the remaining names.

"What about Isaiah, the Alpha of Passion?" Adrian asks, ready to cross the name off.

I think about it for a moment. "I don't see why not."

Adrian raises an eyebrow.

"What? I'm passionate."

He leaves the name uncrossed.

"What about Jasper? Alpha of Devotion." Adrian muses. I bite my lip. Not an option.

"He's been missing for years. There's no way that's even plausible," I tell him. The Devotion Pack has been almost empty since the Alpha disappeared. Rumours of Phantom Wolves roaming around scared Pack members away.

Adrian crosses him from the list.

"How about Grayson?"

I hesitate, lifting my head from where I was brushing lint off my jeans.

"Who's that again?" I ask. The name Grayson doesn't ring a bell, which is strange, since I'm familiar with most Alphas.

"Alpha of Freedom," Adrian reminds me.

I slip off the edge of the desk and take the pen from Adrian's hand. I proceed to draw a thick, red line over the name. Adrian stares at me as I resume my spot.

"Explanation?"

"Easy. I'm from the Discipline Pack. We like order, sense, and reason. He's from the Freedom Pack. They are advocators of the wild and the senseless," I reply as I cross my arms around my chest. Fate is cruel, but he isn't *that* cruel.

Adrian sighs deeply and we collectively stare at the name.

"There's always a chance the Moon Goddess wanted to see if a pairing like that could coexist," Adrian muses.

He knows nothing about the Moon Goddess. While my original Pack worshiped her to an extent, his Pack insisted she didn't exist. I'm indifferent.

Adrian notices my expression. "What? There's a science in love too."

Rolling my eyes, I quickly sum up the remaining Alphas. There are not many left to narrow down from. I notice Adrian's gaze linger over Alpha Grayson's name.

"Don't worry, there is no way Grayson is my mate."

Chapter One

"You look great," Adrian murmurs as he fixes the collar of my blouse. My jaw clenches as his fingers fiddle with the thick fabric. A massive crowd of people stand on the opposite side of the thin curtain, and the sound of them mulling around is making me nervous.

Adrian pauses as he notices my gaze wander.

"Be careful out there," he tells me, stepping back.

"Why? It's just another speech about taking down the Alphas." Everyone here hates the Alphas. Sure, I agree with my own words, but Kaden watches me carefully at all times.

"People are starting to get suspicious. They are wondering why, whatever you say, Kaden manages to answer with some sort of cunning plan," Adrian says.

I close my eyes. It has never been my intention to play them. Nothing more appeals to me than dragging an Alpha down, but what I can't tell these people is that if there is any wrong move on my part, Kaden will have me killed.

"Whether it's a raid on a major public building, or a protest outside his estate, you say, he answers," Adrian says sternly, but his words don't affect me. I know this. He's right in every way, but there is nothing I can do to stop it.

"I know, I know," I say as I throw my hands up. I turn around, facing the curtain that leads onto the stage. Of course, I know. It haunts me every night.

Without another word, I push through the black cloth, revealing myself to the thick crowd of bustling people. Instantly, heads turn and submissiveness settles over them. This must be what it feels like to be an Alpha.

My strides are confident as I find the centre of the stage. This is what I enjoy. Not the attention, more like the sense of order that finds these criminals the moment I am in their presence.

"Thank you for coming." My voice carries over the shadowed faces in the crowd. I try not to make eye contact with anyone specifically. Instead, I try to address them with one sweeping gaze of the courtyard.

My speeches have become a sort of tradition. Many have told me themselves that I bring a familiarity to the bleakness. This place is like a prison, with walls tall and consuming. I don't mind it. Call me institutionalized, but I've begun to rely on these walls.

"Protests are going well, and I believe we are making progress," I tell them. I don't need a microphone. My words radiate off the silence like a speaker.

Someone coughs, but I ignore them. "In no time, we will be leading this Pack collectively!"

This time, people cheer. That's what they want to hear. They want to rule, and they will. What Kaden doesn't know is that there is more of this rebellion going on behind the scenes. Some of it, even I don't have a handle on.

When it comes to my overall goal, I want to find my mate and take over his Pack. People shouldn't be born into power! No matter what Pack it is. Even so, if my dream doesn't come to fruition, there are people that will mount my head to the wall if I don't obey them.

"We will not stand for oppression!"

People surge forward, trying to get closer to me on the stage. I don't take a step back. I won't be intimidated by own kind.

"We will not be shut down by these self-entitled men that call themselves Alphas!"

Passion surges in my veins. It expresses itself in my voice, my movement, and my entire being. What they don't realize is that it is a trap.

Except for one.

He stands at the front of the crowd. My heart stops and I feel paralyzed from the neck down. The color of his eyes is unique. For a moment, it flickers through my mind that he could control me if he wanted to. However, that is not what he is after. It is something else. The way he looks at me is puzzling.

Is it out of frustration, or admiration?

I glide my gaze over him, from the silkiest head of obsidian hair, to his strong jawline. I don't allow myself to glance at his body. Instead, I look up, trying to regain my composure.

At that moment, I realize I can't go on. There is an Alpha here.

"I... I... I..." My words stumble over each other, my equilibrium thrown off from his presence. Everyone stares at me expectantly, including him.

"Well..."

Why am I struggling find my words?

"She's a fake!" Someone yells from the crowd.

I suddenly see a single man pushing his way through the crowd. He shoulders past the Alpha, causing a look of confusion to cast across his face. All I can do is concentrate on this stranger as he accelerates towards the stage.

"We know you are working with Kaden," the man spits, climbing over the edge of the stage. No one has ever bothered assigning guards to me at these events. We never really saw the point since I thought everyone was on my side.

I guess not.

"I'm not..." I whisper, hoping no one can hear the fear in my voice.

No one stops him as he crawls up onto the stage. Before I can react, he is standing inches from my face, staring at me with hands clenched at his sides, breathing heavily. His isn't just mad, he's livid.

"Hey buddy," someone says from behind the man. "I don't think you should get any closer to this lady here."

The strange Alpha I've never seen before is clutching the stranger's shoulder. His eyes are staring directly at me, despite his words being directed at the stranger.

"Don't you see what she's doing? She's lying to us!" The stranger yells, probably wishing he were taller, since his height hardly compares to the Alpha. Before any further action is taken, someone grabs my arm and begins dragging me backward.

"We need to get you out of here," I hear Adrian say in my ear. His hand on my arm pulls me behind the curtain, sheltering me from the chants from the crowd outside.

Once I'm fully concealed, Adrian lets me go.

"Why the hell is there an Alpha out there?" I question as I run my hands through my hair. I just completely embarrassed myself. I have never been so flustered, but the moment I saw the Alpha, I couldn't move. I became an incoherent mess, and I hate myself for it.

"An Alpha?"

Clearly, Adrian didn't see him. "There's an Alpha out there! He heard everything!"

He must think I'm such a freak. I was talking about overpowering the Alphas, and he still stood up for me when that stranger rushed the stage. Sure, I can look after myself, but I don't want my slowly thinning number of followers to get any fewer by watching me fight a protestor. It will diminish any respect that I've gained from them.

"What Alpha?" Adrian questions with shockingly wide eyes. Closing my eyes, I remember *exactly* how he looked. The image of him is imprinted in my mind.

"I don't know," I mutter honestly. "He had silver eyes like I've never seen before."

Adrian pauses. His expression suggests I just told him the most shocking news, and he's struggling to grasp it.

"That's Grayson, Lexia," Adrian insists, making my heart sink in my chest.

"Grayson, as in the Alpha of Freedom?" That man is the last Alpha I want to have here right now. I would have preferred Noah, Alpha of Harmony, to be at this speech despite the way it went.

"Alpha of Freedom indeed," a soft, silky voice says from behind me. I spin around, desperate to see who owns that beautiful voice.

As I turn, glancing over my shoulder, my eyes meet those silver ones again.

Chapter Two

I've never been this terrified in my life. Not only is it the fact that an Alpha is standing inches away from me, but that he is staring directly at me, as if unaffected by the words I just uttered out there on stage. His expression is so impassive.

"What are you doing here?" I question. I'm surprised that the words even come out of my mouth.

His mouth curves up into a slight smile. "I wanted to talk to you," he says smoothly, tilting his head ever so slightly.

Adrian suddenly steps forward, grabbing my arm gently in his hand. He is the complete opposite of me in this situation, remaining calm and professional. My bet is that I am probably bright red. My hands are shaking by my sides.

"She has a private office," Adrian says, stepping up to his role of assistant at the one time I don't appreciate. All I want to do is tell Alpha Grayson to leave so I don't have to face this current embarrassment.

For a moment, I want to question the way Grayson stares pointedly at Adrian's hand on my arm, but I brush it away. Grayson nods, accepting the idea of meeting in my office. Internally, I curse Adrian's entire existence.

Leading the way, I guide Grayson to my office with Adrian in tow. The upgraded warehouse I call home and work seems to be very interesting to the Alpha. His eyes catch on everything we pass by, and I hope for a moment he doesn't notice the fingers crossed at my side. I am secretly hoping I don't make a fool of myself further.

Adrian offers Grayson some water. "I'm fine, thank you," Grayson says. He sits on the other side of the desk from me, staring at me so blatantly I can't keep eye contact without squirming. There is something about the silver of his eyes that unnerves me.

Adrian leaves the room, leaving Grayson and I alone.

Grayson sits forward abruptly. "Is he your mate?"

"What?" I stutter, his words taking me by surprise.

"Or your boyfriend? Or your partner?" he demands, his gaze relentless. His eyebrow rises as he stares expectantly at me for an answer. I attempt to gather my bearings.

"He is just my assistant."

He pauses, narrowing his eyes. Slowly, he leans back again, but he doesn't dare take his gaze off me.

"Assistant in what? Sexual favo…"

I cough, cutting him off. *Why is he talking about this?*

"Let's not talk about this," I suggest as I shuffle papers around on my desk. I feel a sheen of sweat gathering on my forehead.

"You should have saved yourself for your mate!" We stare into each other's eyes.

"You're very intrusive, aren't you?" I mutter, lowering my gaze.

"I don't think your mate would be very happy about the way that man looks at you."

I snap my head up, furiously glaring at him. "It's just casual sex. Nothing more, nothing less."

This shuts him up. His mouth sets in a firm line, and he slowly leans forward. It's true. What Adrian and I have isn't love, it's sex, and that is all I want. No complications and no worry about mates.

"You're too beautiful to be having mindless sex with a man like him," Grayson muses. I hate how serious he sounds. It makes me think for a second that he means it.

"Look, I am not about to take advice from an Alpha," I growl, my hands clenching underneath my desk. He smiles gently, but a slight haze of bitterness still shrouds his gaze.

I watch him sigh. "Your true mate would worship you, in and out of bed."

"What would you know about my mate?" I mutter sourly.

He pauses.

Closing my eyes, I draw in a shaky breath and imagine the red line crossed through his name. He is not my mate. We are opposites in every way possible. The Moon Goddess isn't that stupid...

"Can we talk about why you're really here, please?"

Grayson hesitates for another moment before responding. "I have a proposal for you, and please don't make a rash decision."

"Okay..."

"I want you to come and work with me," he says with anxiety in his voice.

I pause. His words are so surprising to me that I almost topple back in my chair.

"With you? As in, a partner?" I rephrase, trying to make sense of the entire situation. How could he be saying these things after seeing me completely degrade the existence of Alphas on that stage?

"Yes, Lexia. I need a partner to control an army of mine. I saw your leadership skills, and I think you're fully capable of leading my people."

The words he is telling me have completely wiped away any sense of control I have been able to salvage over the past 10 minutes. I can hardly breathe, even as he stares at me with a soothing look in his eyes.

"You're kidding?" I sputter. He must be.

"No. Kaden recommended me to you himself. He tells me you are incredibly capable of leading an entire army yourself. I hope you will consider my proposal with an open mind."

The way he announces this is so casual, as if he's reciting a mantra he's used to every day. Maybe it's because he's from the Freedom Pack, and he doesn't have to worry about anything.

"That son of a bitch," I growl, standing up from my seat. "He just wants to get rid of me!"

Grayson frowns. "Do you not think you are capable?"

"It's not that... I can't do this, I'm sorry," I tell him. I'm not sure why I am apologizing to him, considering I've never wanted to aid an Alpha in my entire life. I have to admit, collaborating with an Alpha would give me significant step forward. I would gain inside access to his Pack, meaning I wouldn't have to bother finding my mate.

"You don't have to give me an answer now, but please Lexia, I need you… to help me."

He stands cautiously, either waiting for me to yell at him to leave, or to gracelessly accept his offer. The latter is not one I'm ready to agree to just yet. I can't abandon the people I'm leading right now without serious consideration.

"I will," I promise, finally sounding more normal to him than I ever have before.

We gaze at each other for a few dazzled moments, before he turns and walks from the room.

***

"You'd be an idiot not to do it," Adrian says.

We sit in my bedroom, a couple hours after Grayson has left. He came in like a storm, and has left this odd calm behind that has left me thinking about his offer. As tempting as it sounds, I'm still not sure I should even be considering it right now.

"What about my people? I'll be leaving them behind," I tell him. He shakes his head, pacing the room a little bit.

"Think of it like this. It won't be forever and I'll babysit them while you're gone," he says with a humorous smile. I roll my eyes. Like he'd be capable of looking after this Pack of criminals.

"Look, we need to concentrate on what's happening in the next three days," Adrian says, clapping his hands together.

He seems to notice my expression. "Remember? I got you tickets to a special function Saturday night."

"Function?"

"The Alphas hold this soirée every year, and I managed to get you a ticket. We have a job to do, and it's going to happen…"

12

My head is spinning. Alpha Grayson shows up here in the middle of one of my speeches, and I can't seem to get over his presence.

I try to gain some composure. "Explain?"

"Alpha Noah is the Alpha of Harmony. He knows every Pack's weakness, and I need you to find out the Vengeance Pack's one by…"

He breaks off and instantly I know what he is insinuating. He wants me to seduce Alpha Noah. It's not the first time I've done this type of mission, but never with an Alpha.

"Will Grayson be there?" I ask. His nod makes me cringe.

"Every Alpha will be there. Let's hope you're good at avoiding ones of the Freedom Pack."

Chapter Three

"You look beautiful by the way," Adrian murmurs as he helps me out of the car.

Ignoring him, I smooth out my dress, gazing around at the beautiful view. Isaiah, the Alpha of Passion, is hosting this party. Despite his Pack not being in the best condition, he still holds the most lavish party every year.

"You don't mind, do you?" I ask anxiously, still looking at Isaiah's estate. People are mulling around, finding their way in at their own pace. Guards stand post in nearly every shadow I glance at, and all of them are watching us with careful eyes.

"Mind what?"

"What I have to do tonight?" I say, folding my arms across my chest.

Looking around, I take in what a shame it is that Alpha Isaiah's Pack went rogue a few years ago. Every one of them rebelled and he has had a hard time trying to rein them back in. Hence, the collaboration with the Alpha of Discipline.

"It's fine, Lexia. It's work and it's not like we are dating anyway," he assures me. I glance down, staring at how the silver of my dress glimmers under the moonlight. Adrian reaches out, handing me my ticket.

"Try not to get distracted. Get to Alpha Noah, find out what you need to know, and get out of there," Adrian instructs. I nod, affirming I know the plan.

Twisting around, I walk alone towards the double doors of Isaiah's estate. The gritty smell of the sea is present, as is the sound of waves lapping on the shore. The Passion Pack is the only coastal Pack, and I am not used to it. The Vengeance Pack is one of the cooler Packs, to the South, while this Pack is up North where it is tropical.

I make it in to the party without too much hassle. No one bothers asking who I am, and I slip through the crowd unnoticed. I have a mild back story just in case someone decides to approach me. I doubt I will have to use it since everyone is distracted by the presence of Alphas.

I swerve my way through people on the dance floor, mumbling 'excuse me', and 'sorry' as I go. The crowd begins to thin out and my eyes scan the area. I try not to get distracted by the extravagant outfits people are wearing. My goal is to find Alpha Noah.

Turns out, Alpha Noah is tucked in a corner talking to two very official-looking people in suits. Annoyed, I wade my way back onto the busy dance floor, keeping my eye on him the entire time.

Like most Alphas, he is naturally handsome. His blond hair is thick, contrasting with his naturally tan skin. His eyes are similar to mine, but so much different; a much lighter, glowing green that sparks as he assesses the man in front of him.

Suddenly, as I blindly walk, keeping my attention fixed on Noah, I smack straight into someone's back.

Stumbling backward, I blink a few times, having managed to lose my bearings. The man who I smacked my forehead into didn't even turn around. In fact, he continued to talk to the lovely women in front of him.

Scowling at the back of his black suit, I resist the urge to punch him. Sure, I should have been looking where I was going, but he could have at least excused himself. I tap his broad shoulder, not being able to smother the glare on my face.

Instantly, it melts away as he turns around. Here I stand, facing one of the most beautiful men I have ever laid my eyes on. Definitely an Alpha.

"May I help you?" he questions. His voice is so smooth and sensual it caresses my skin, forcing me to suppress a shiver. Eyes of deep-set, swirling violet and ebony dance across my entire body, observing me silently. Eyes so illusory and mystical I find myself questioning if he is real.

"Sorry," I mutter, retreating a few steps in a mixture of awe and fear.

Shadowy wisps of dark hair scatter across his sun-kissed forehead, almost covering those deceptive eyes. I am not sure if it is the lights or my eyes, but his black hair seems to have a violet tint, but only a trace. I expect him to turn around again, especially since he is occupied with women exceptionally more beautiful than I am.

Instead, the elusive man reaches out with long arms, grabbing my forearms between his soft hands. I'm trapped. Not because I can't move from his grip, but because his gaze has me pinned to the spot.

"Why are you sorry? You requested my attention and I am obliging," he says as he raises a dark eyebrow.

I can't stop staring at him. Whoever he is, he is an Alpha and I can't think which one.

"Did you not feel me run into you?" I question, salvaging my voice from the ruins of embarrassment I just created. He frowns, his smooth forehead creasing in confusion. By the look on his face, he didn't feel my entire head rebound off his spine.

As if my words triggered something in the universe, someone hits me in the back. I lurch forward, stumbling toward the man in front of me. His grip on me only tightens as he swings me to his side.

I am suddenly facing the other person. It is a drunk man who winks at me before wandering off into the crowd.

"We should expect nothing less being on the dance floor," the Alpha muses, easily casting a fleeting gaze across the room with his height. Of course, he is right, but this had been my best vantage point of Noah.

Suddenly, remembering my mission, I look over to see if Noah is where I last saw him.

"You interrupted my time with those ladies. I believe you owe me a dance," the Alpha proclaims, gazing at me through the tendrils of his dark hair.

I cock my head, taken by surprise at his sudden proposal. His words seem to insinuate the start of a new song, the lyrics sung in

16

foreign words and carried by the sweetest melody. His hand swings out from behind his back, all bare and inviting. On a whim, I slide my hand into his, enticed by music, his violet eyes, and the atmosphere.

He leads me deeper into the crowd, immersing us in the moment. As he glides so exquisitely among the people, going unnoticed by them despite his stand-alone beauty, I follow. I am enchanted by his peculiar spell, especially as he sweeps me into a common waltzing embrace, consuming me with just one flicker of a smile.

"Who are you?" My voice seems loud between us. Whoever he is, he has cast magic upon me, and there is no way I can escape. If I could, I am not sure I would want to.

For a moment, he doesn't answer. Swaying to the sound of music, I concentrate on him. Perhaps if I wasn't drunk on the moment, I would pay more attention to the shadows that seem to surround us. He brings me closer to him and whispers in my ear, "Jasper."

"The Alpha of Devotion?" I ask breathlessly. It strikes me that I don't doubt it, but I should. It should be impossible that I am dancing in his arms right now.

"You're clever," he says.

"But the Alpha of Devotion has been missing for years."

Alpha Jasper disappeared into the darkness and never came back. Rumours were that he was kidnapped and murdered by Phantom Wolves, but here he stands. Beautifully dressed and staring down at me with those unique-colored eyes.

"Am I?" Jasper asks, amused. The weight of his hand on my waist suddenly becomes apparent.

"If you're really Jasper, then why isn't everyone celebrating your return?" I decide to ask. He tilts his head and takes my hand in his. He spins me in a tight circle as the music changes. As the turn ends, he captures me in his arms again.

He shrugs. "Maybe I never left."

"What do you mean?" I ask curiously. We sidestep another couple as they laugh and stumble around like idiots drunk on love.

"I think this is a conversation for another time, Lexia," he says softly.

I flinch, retreating a few steps, slipping from his grip.

Instead of me being worried by the fact that he knows my name, he grins at me with a careless half-smile, but his cunning eyes suggest he knows *exactly* what he is doing. He takes another step forward, but I match it back.

"How do you know my name?" I demand, a sudden fear sparking inside me. The enchantment I was enraptured in is extinguished.

Instead of answering me, Jasper glances over his shoulder. I follow his gaze to see Grayson shouldering his way through the crowd.

"I shall see you later tonight, Lexia," Jasper says quickly before strolling casually past me. I twist around to witness him go, only to see he has vanished without a trace into the mass of people.

"Lexia? What the hell are you doing here?"

I feel a hand on my shoulder, making me turn. Grayson stands directly in front of me, looking handsome as ever. His dark suit makes him look so dazzling, as well as his tie and paper-thin gloves. He runs his gaze over me, not bothering to keep his observations to himself.

"I was just with Jasper," I find myself saying. Grayson furrows his brow in confusion.

Seeing him standing in front of me, all dressed up, is overwhelming, as is the urge to touch him. I brush the thought away, trying to concentrate on what he is saying.

"Jasper is gone and he isn't coming back," Grayson tells me. Now, it's my time to be confused. I definitely didn't imagine Jasper here moments ago, even though it felt unreal. I am positive I saw Grayson look straight at us.

"He and I were literally just dancing together," I insist, running a hand down my face in bitter annoyance.

Grayson grabs my bare arm, his soft glove being the only thing between us. "You'd better not be drunk, Lexia."

I gape at him in disbelief. I am not sure if I should waste my time on lecturing him about me being drunk. Frankly, it is none of his business if I was drinking anyway. That isn't what is worrying me.

He didn't see Jasper, but I did...

Chapter Four

"Listen, you shouldn't be here," Grayson insists, glancing around as if someone might see him talking to a negligible such as me. I roll my eyes, brushing past him, only to be followed closely.

He grabs my arm, forcing me to give him my full attention. "You could at least tell me why you're here."

I narrow my eyes at him. What business is it of his what I do? Sure, it's obvious I am not wanted here, a party where Alphas mingle with other high bloods. That is where my back story comes in; I am the daughter of a rich executive who lives in the hills of the Discipline Pack. That way, no one would question my indigenous eye color. However, my back story doesn't work with Grayson. He knows who I am and what hatred I have toward Alphas. He knows I am a risk, so any excuse I can conjure up is sure to be useless.

"Why I am here is none of your business," I snap, narrowing my eyes on the hand still firmly clutching my arm. His gloves are similar to those other men here wear. It is uncommon for unmated males to go without gloves to parties like these, especially Alphas. This is mainly because parties like these are for men and women to party without the worry of finding their mate.

"It is, if you're conspiring against one of us," Grayson says. By the look in his eyes, he doesn't want to believe the words he is saying, but he knows he is correct in his assumptions.

I nod down to his hand on my arm. "I think you should let me go."

Looking at his hand, I suddenly notice something glint around his finger through the thin fabric of his glove. It looks to be a silver ring.

"Why the hell are you wearing a silver ring?" I question. Silver burns, so he should be in pain right now.

He swallows. "I…"

"Just let me go," I insist again, desperate to get away from him.

"Lexia," he says, his voice thick with warning. I twist my arm from his grip, taking a step back.

"Don't come near me ever again," I growl. "And consider your offer declined."

It feels good to turn around and walk away from him with my departing words. Even though his angered gaze on my back is heavy, and I might regret making enemies with an Alpha, it still feels exhilarating.

I weave my way past dancing bodies, trying to find the outskirts so I can breathe.

"Hello Blondie, what brings you here?"

The slurred sound of a drunken idiot makes me pause, but not just any drunken idiot. A Love Pack idiot. You can tell by their strong accents that allude to their bedroom desires.

"Malik," I mutter sourly. I would know those glassy blue eyes anywhere.

"As much as I love you in that dress, I would love it more to see you out of it," Malik says. His mouth tilts into a suggestive smile.

There is no way I am in the mood for his romantic tendencies. Unmated Love Pack members are the worst. "Aren't there plenty of drunk, unmated females for you to seduce elsewhere?" I question, setting my voice into a bored tone so he will get the hint that I am not interested in whatever he is offering.

"I've never been with a girl from the Discipline Pack. Are they as wild as I hear?" Malik asks as he takes a shaky step closer to me.

The way he looks at me through strands of ruffled brown hair suddenly makes me nervous. He is serious, and by the way his hand twitches slightly by his side, it is obvious he is itching to get his hands on someone. I happen to be the closest.

"You should go, Malik, I'm not interested," I caution. He only chuckles, taking yet another step closer, which I match back.

"Lexia, we should be going," a smooth, caressing voice utters from behind me. I don't even have to bother turning around to know it is Jasper.

Malik looks blandly at Jasper, who stands behind me. No flicker of recognition sparks in his eyes, as if he doesn't realize he is staring at the long-lost Alpha of Devotion. Maybe he is just too drunk.

"You're her date?" Malik questions, finally taking a step backward. The relief that I feel is overwhelming and so is the desire to turn around to thank Jasper. Sure, Malik would have been on the floor holding his privates had he advanced any closer, but another failed relationship with an Alpha wouldn't be good.

Jasper must have nodded, as he grabs my hand and Malik backs off. All of a sudden, as if he has spotted another lone girl to prowl on, Malik disappears into the crowd.

"Thank you," I say, as I turn around, facing Jasper. I can feel sweat dripping down my cheek.

"You look hot. Come and get a drink," Jasper says, nodding his head toward the bar. A drink of water doesn't sound terrible right now, especially with the heat and the clinginess of my dress.

Together, we walk to the bar and take a seat on two barstools. Jasper offers a glass of water that was already sitting there. Nervously, I take a sip. Tastes like water.

"He wanted you, badly," Jasper mutters, his back facing the bar as he stares out into the crowd. "He isn't the only one."

"Don't tell me you only saved me from Malik as a way to get in my pants," I say, gladly joking. Although Jasper seems to take it very seriously.

"I'm not interested in you, Lexia. Especially not with your mate here."

His words spark an interest in me. The mention of him knowing my mate has me curious, especially since he is an Alpha.

"And your mate?" I ask.

Jasper's eyes shadow and instantly I know the subject is a little shady. "We aren't together."

"Why not?" I should really shut up.

"She doesn't believe I exist."

I bite back another question. By the look on Jasper's face, he isn't so happy about the thought of his mate.

"Malik didn't notice me," Jasper stated, bringing the subject up that I had been meaning to ask.

I take another sip of my water. "Why not?"

Jasper shrugs, but he holds back his reason. He seems to be enjoying this elusive set of questions, and denying me the answers. All these loose ends are making me nervous.

"How do you know my name?"

He tilts his head as I stare at him over the rim of my glass.

"It's not that hard to learn someone's name," he muses.

My jaw clenches and I set my drink down. I suppose he's right, but why would he go out of his way to find out my name when he and I hadn't met until an hour ago? Surely, he didn't know I existed until I tapped on his back. I was about to bring up my valid argument, when he cut me off with his own words.

"What you should be worried about is why I know you truly don't want a mate," Jasper added. "You're scared of whoever he might be, but you're mainly scared that he will abandon you like your sister's mate did when she was killed by those men..."

My heart skips a beat.

His words burn into the truth that surrounds them. He's right. He is so right, and it makes me sick. I've never told anyone that in my life...

"How did you know?" I question, my voice shaky and unsure.

Jasper leans forward in his seat, a slight smile of wicked knowledge etched into his face. He truly isn't normal. He reaches out his arm, and with the tip of his index finger, he brushes his fingertip along my temple.

"Because you told me."

Chapter Five

No. It's not possible.

Jasper stares at me, waiting for some sort of reaction, but I keep my expression impassive. He *must* be joking with me. Mind readers don't exist...

"We do exist, quite frankly," Jasper says casually, raising a darkened eyebrow at me.

I flinch.

"Listen, I have many powers and the reason why is something I can't discuss with you right now. Which is why..."

"You're a Phantom Wolf?" I blurt out.

Instantly, Jasper's face darkens. I don't know why I mentioned it, but it seems to be the only possible way to get a reaction out of him. My reasoning behind it isn't just because of the mind reading business.

"I said, we *can't* talk about it here," Jasper repeats, his jaw tightening.

I was right and no matter how hard my conscious, realistic thoughts try to tell me that Phantom Wolves don't exist, something in the back of my mind hints at the opposite.

"I know it's hard to believe, but trust me, you need to take this drink," he mutters, suddenly sliding a glass of red wine across the tabletop. Where had that come from? I don't remembering seeing the bartender conjure it up. I hold the stem of the glass warily between my fingertips.

"After what you've just told me, I think I won't take this drink from you," I tell him shakily, without breaking his relentless eye contact.

"Drink, it's not spiked," Jasper insists.

This man is either telling the truth, which is on the high end of the spectrum, or he's crazy, and wants any reason to get away with spiking my drink.

I stare at the inside of the glass that is filled with swirls of red, foreign wine. It looks so tempting, but I still don't trust Jasper.

"You're not really a Phantom Wolf though. I've heard they are deformed creatures that only come out at night," I tell him, glancing around for my nearest escape route.

Jasper suddenly holds his hand up, showing me something I never noticed before: a silver ring, practically burning into his skin. It looks so familiar, aside from the markings engraved in it: *Commander of the Night.*

"If you drink this, I'll explain everything," Jasper promises.

My mind swirls with unanswered questions and crazy, delusional men. He claims to read my mind, and has done a good job of it thus far, although my mind doesn't seem to grasp the impossible idea.

As I take a sip of the cool liquid, I wonder if that's his plan. Give me alcohol so I'm calmer when he breaks it to me that he's a mass-murdering Phantom, or something much worse.

Instead, as I lower the glass, the wine is gone and has been replaced with a thick, black liquid. My glass falls from my hand in a fright, shattering on the tabletop. Rather than splashing across the wood, the liquid vanishes.

"Did you poison me?" I growl, stumbling off my chair. Jasper stands looking slightly solemn with his choices, but still grasps my arm firmly.

"No, it's not poison. Just stay here and wait for the effects to set in," he says softly, but I rip away from him.

"You're crazy..." I mutter. The effects of whatever I drank start to form a haze around the edges of my vision. Again, Jasper makes a reach for me, but I dodge him.

He sighs. "Please, Lexia, it's in your best interest."

24

His words carry away as I find myself stumbling across the dance floor, hardly controlling my own feet anymore. I can't leave here until I have completed the mission, which means I need to find Noah.

Emerging from the crowd, my eyes land on Noah, the man I came here for, and I realize the opportunity to approach him is perfect. No one is near him as he stares out of the wide window at the end of the room, observing the night.

"Alpha Noah," I slur, a stupid smile on my face.

He turns, green eyes seeking out my own. He doesn't recognize me, which doesn't surprise me. I would be worried if he did. His eyes seem to light up when he sees me, obviously somewhat interested in what I have to say. Although, I'm sure he's used to women coming up to him all the time.

"Yes?" Noah says, turning to face me.

"You're very attractive," I stutter, everyone around us seeming to vanish. All I see is the confusion in his eyes.

Complete the mission. Get out of here before the drugs render me useless.

Before I can stop myself, part of my brain is suddenly controlled by whatever magic Jasper wields. I fall into Noah, who catches me adeptly.

"Are you okay?" He asks, his voice rough and husky. An Alpha, especially one of Harmony, would jump at any occasion to assist someone. His hands feel strange on my arms as he tries to steady me. If I had control over myself right now, I would turn around and run in the opposite direction. This mission needs to be completed, or I'll never be able to look Adrian in the eye again.

"I think I like you." The words come out of my mouth before I can stop them.

He smiles, showing me he is rather handsome. "Someone's drunk."

I brush my finger against his chin. To my dismay, he doesn't object. Is this what Jasper wants? At least I can confirm Alpha Noah is not my mate. His hands are on my waist, as if he's having a hard time controlling himself. Suddenly, he leans down, mouth by my ear.

"I want to take you to bed," he whispers. Usually girls throw themselves at other Alphas, such as Malik, the Alpha of Love, and Isaiah, the Alpha of Passion. They don't want the Alpha of Loyalty or Harmony in bed with them.

Complete the mission. Get out of here before the drugs render me useless.

Everything is spinning and my eyes feel like they want to close.

He grabs my hand and turns me toward the exit, but stops abruptly at the sight of another Alpha in front of him. Unsure of what he's doing, I tilt my head around his body to see through the cloudy haze of swirling drunkenness.

"Where are you going?" Grayson questions Noah, as if I don't exist. *When did he get here?*

I can't really see him properly, but I know it's him. The dark suit, dishevelled hair, and silver eyes blur together in color, but the aura he seems to admit makes sense to my body. I hate that fact.

"Grayson... I was... ah..."

"Sorry to interrupt you. Were you two going somewhere?" Grayson asks while looking straight at me. I rub my eyes, wishing I didn't feel like vomiting straight onto the floor.

"Just upstairs."

Upstairs. Everyone at this party knows what upstairs means. If my eyes aren't deceiving me, Grayson's face seems to shutter at the utterance of the word.

"I don't think that's a good idea," he says darkly.

"Why not?" Noah questions, sounding a little frustrated with Grayson's interference.

Noah goes to push past him, dragging me along with him, but Grayson pushes his shoulder back. Hard.

"I said, I don't think that's a good idea."

Like a switch, my vision seems to have repaired itself enough to witness the anger on Grayson's face. I've never seen him like this before, even after I declined his offer. Such a dark, menacing expression directed at Noah.

"What's your problem?" Noah questions, his voice raised in annoyance.

"I warned you and you didn't listen."

What is he doing? It's none of Grayson's business what I do, and at this point, he's ruining my mission. I step up right between the two threatening Alphas.

"Grayson, back off," I growl.

Something sparks in his eyes. Something that expresses his rank as Alpha better than I could ever explain.

"Yeah man, or show this entire place what you really are," Noah says, his voice taunting. *What he really is?*

Noah pushes me out of the way gently, but the movement is devastating with my drunken feet. I stumble away, giving the two Alphas the perfect space to confront each other.

Complete the mission. Get out of here before the drugs render me useless.

"I don't think you understand the mistake you're making," Grayson says. Despite the obvious anger radiating under his skin, he's as impassive as ever, facing the situation like a true Alpha.

I know a fight is about to ensue. "Stop!" I yell over the music. Not many people take notice, but the two men do. At that exact moment, the drugs hit me like a truck, and I stumble a little on my feet.

"I think I'm going to pass out…"

I don't know whose arms I land in until I force my heavy lids open to see a pair of frightened silver eyes looking straight back at me.

Chapter Six

The first breath of consciousness I have is beyond comfortable. So comfortable, in fact, that at first I believe I am floating on a cloud of softness that I never want to escape.

Instead, I'm lying on a bed that's damn well close enough to it, with sheets wrapped around me so soft and silky, they might as well have been tendrils of the sweetest dreams. I don't remember my bed being this nice.

I sit up abruptly, but a pain stabs the upper right half of my head, forcing me back to the pillow. I'm hungover. I don't remember much of last night. Only those violet eyes.

What did I manage to get myself into?

Groaning, I force my wary lids open, glad the curtains around me are drawn. It's light enough outside for me to see the room I'm occupying. I've never seen it in my life.

Lifting the sheets, I glance under. I'm not naked, just stripped to my underwear and bra.

"Thank the Moon Goddess." I mutter, tilting my throbbing head at the ceiling.

I slip out of bed. The air around me is thick and unfamiliar. The room I'm in is decorated so sparsely I'm second hand offended. Who would neglect such a large room with this much potential? Then I remember my home, and shake my head at how much of a hypocrite I am.

I pull back curtains, revealing to me the outside world. I nearly faint at the sight of it. Trees. Then some more trees. And just when you think another mile of trees is just unrealistic, another presents itself. It's so strange, so foreign I want to bundle myself up in those luscious sheets and cry.

A complete change of climate has my head spinning, confusion choking in my throat. How did I get here? I may do some strange things when I drink, but these feet wouldn't carry me across the entire country in one night.

I have to get out of here.

Stumbling back, I rip the top sheet of the bed off, and throw it over my shoulder. Instantly, it sticks to my skin with the heat, like a piece of paper.

The outside of the room is just as strange as the inside, only confirming I've never been here before. I find my way to a flight of steps leading down. As I attempt to find my way to where someone may be, I peek around corners and into rooms. All are completely abandoned. Nothing about this place hints to who owns it.

At the bottom of the steps, a solid door remains closed. My hands tremble as I reach for the knob. A heavy creaking sound fills the corridor as the door opens in front of me. At first glance into the room, I think I am alone. Then, to my horror, I see that someone is standing near the cast iron stove.

His bare, smooth back faces me. His muscles are hardened by movement as he lifts the pan off the flame. He doesn't hear me slip into the room.

Grayson.

Pulling the sheet closer, I pad into the kitchen, slipping onto a stool without him hearing. Why am I here? Did we… No, I don't want to think about it.

I watch him curiously, as he hums an unknown tune. The pan sizzles on the stove. I hate to admit that he is handsome. Although Alphas aren't to my taste, his body is impeccable. I try to push away the image of running my fingernails down his back.

I cough lightly. With spatula in hand, he turns around. "Good morning, Lexia."

I nod toward the spatula in his hand, noticing the grease on it. "What are you cooking?"

Why I decided not acknowledge the obvious elephant in the room, I don't know. Maybe it's because I wanted to keep the conversation light, and not as awkward as it should be.

"Bacon, I hope you're not vegetarian," he says, as if it's an option. I force a smile onto my face.

I watch him fill a glass to the brim with water, and slide it across the bench to me. Every movement he makes is subtle, yet deliberate. Thanking him, I put the glass to my lips, tasting the lukewarm water. He pauses and stares down at me with those mercury eyes.

"Did we sleep together last night?" I ask, cutting to the chase.

Grayson flinches at my words, obviously not expecting them. The only memory I can gather from last night is him, so that's the only conclusion I can come to. As well as the fact that I woke up in his Pack.

"No, we didn't sleep together," he says carefully. "I don't have any interest in being with someone while they are knocked unconscious," Grayson muses. There is a moment of silence as he puts the bacon onto a plate and hands it to me.

"When I do have you in my bed, you're going to be very willing. In fact, you'll be begging," he says with a laugh.

I nearly choke on the not-quite-chewed bacon in my mouth. The way he sounds so casual and sure of himself irritates me. "I… I don't think that's ever going to happen."

"Are you sure? Because I am, and I know for a fact that your little boyfriend would never compare to me in bed," he says, bracing his muscular arms. I avert my gaze and look down at my plate. Here we go with my sex life again.

"He's not my boyfriend."

He raises an eyebrow as if he doesn't believe me, and wills me to stop lying to him. I'm not lying. *Adrian is not my boyfriend.*

"So, he wasn't the one who got you drunk off your face last night?"

Suddenly, things flood into my vision like a tsunami, leaving my mind completely overwhelmed with what happened last night. *Jasper. Noah. Grayson…*

"Someone spiked my drink," I say, making Grayson narrow his eyes speculatively. I remember him not believing me when I told him about Jasper, but I also remember Jasper reading my mind. I declared him to be a Phantom Wolf. If he is, then maybe that's why Grayson couldn't see him. My thoughts are spinning and making me feel nauseous.

"Who?" Grayson demands.

I can't tell him. He won't believe me.

"I don't remember. Look, can you at least tell me why you dragged me all the way back to your Pack?"

He swallows, suddenly looking slightly guilty. He quickly masks it. He seems to be good at that.

"I want you to rethink declining my offer."

So, that's what he wanted. He tried to persuade me when I was unconscious, thinking that bringing me back to his Pack would seal the deal.

"I told you, I'm not interested," I mutter, pushing my plate away. Grayson watches me carefully as I stand, the bench being the only barrier between us.

"Why? This is what you want, isn't it? To be a leader? What's better than being an equal to an Alpha?" His words bite at the emotional wall I've put up to protect myself.

I sigh, running a hand irritably through my hair. It's so tempting. So damn unrealistic, yet plausible enough that I might as well reach out and grab it.

"I can't abandon the people back in my Pack," I tell him firmly.

"I've sent four capable men to deal with that situation."

My mouth falls open. *He what?*

"I'm sorry, why didn't you just hire those four men to do this job?" I question.

He goes silent at this. He places his hand slowly down on the bench between us. His fingertips brush against the surface as he comes a little closer. Instantly, my pulse quickens.

31

"Because, there's something about you that I *really* like and I need. I've seen how you lead, and my Pack needs you, Lexia," he says.

The way my name glides off his tongue with such exotic smoothness has me stunned. He doesn't stop his floating-like steps until he is right in front of me. I can smell the fresh spice coming off him.

"At least see the Pack first. At least get a feel for the people you may lead before you go back," he murmurs.

I'm not sure what willed me to do it.

Chapter Seven

"We could go out now, if you would like, to see the Pack," Grayson offers. I accept after finishing my plate. He takes the empty plate from me, and slides it into the sink.

I glance outside, shaking my head. "I don't think I can handle the heat."

It's true. One step outside, and I'm positive I might faint. It's not because I can't usually handle the heat, but I'm still coming down from the effects of the drug Jasper gave me. Thank the Moon Goddess I didn't stay around to find out what *he* wanted.

"What about this evening?" I ask.

Instantly, it's as if I've pushed a button labelled *don't touch*. He stiffens, his gaze growing cold and rigid.

"I don't think that's going to work," he says softly. The way it sounds is as if he's in pain, as if he's fighting off an inner demon.

"Maybe by tomorrow I'll be over this drug and we can go," I say nervously, hoping I'm not pushing too far. I had accepted his offer to continue my mission to take over an Alpha's position, and achieve the goal of democracy throughout the Packs. His sudden shift in mood has me a little nervous.

"Good idea," he replies, looking up through his dark hair and meeting my gaze. Something about his eyes always stops my heart for a second.

I excuse myself, dragging the blanket over my shoulders back up to the room. I need time to think about this, but ultimately, I can't shake the fact that Grayson is hiding something big from me.

The moment I step back into the bedroom, I notice a piece of clothing lying on the bed. At closer inspection, it's a simple large shirt. A man's shirt, with a little handwritten note on it.

All I have, sorry.

Did I stumble into the wrong room, or did Grayson manage to get a shirt up here so quickly I didn't even notice? Perhaps he has people to do it for him. He's an Alpha, I suppose.

I scrunch the note up in my hand and toss it back onto the bed. Since the shirt is nice and big, maybe it won't be so hot. Hoping I'm right, I shrug the blanket off myself and slip his shirt on. It even smells like him.

I fall face-first into the bed, wondering if maybe I could catch a nap until it's cooler outside. Instead, I'm hit in the face with another note. This time, it is stuck to the pillow. Peeling it off my face, I inspect the completely different handwriting.

Meet me outside, now. Jasper

This means answers. Answers to so many things I've been desperate to find out. The idea of clarity has me on my feet in excitement. At the same time, this may possibly be a trap, or a way for Jasper to finish the mission he started. The rewards outweigh the risk.

Following the only route in this place that I know, I go down the stairs and back into the kitchen, where I remember seeing a back door.

To my dismay, Grayson is still here. He is standing with his back to me facing the sink, and the only thing he is wearing is a pair of black dish gloves. One brief eyeful of a very firm, smooth butt has me ducking for cover behind the bench.

"Is that you, Lexia?"

I press myself as close to the bench as physics allow. He can't see me, but I see him.

I hear his footsteps getting closer, and I squeeze my eyes shut in the hope that I won't have to see any more of him naked. Suddenly, the feel of his rubber gloves on my skin makes me jump. *He's right there, and he's naked.*

"I didn't know you were shy," he says, his voice light with a chuckle.

How dare he be amused! Who just walks around without any clothes on with others in his house? Alphas of Freedom, obviously.

"Sorry, I don't want your *thing* in my face," I growl, shielding my eyes with my hand.

His laugh becomes animated. "My *thing*? You mean my…"

"Shut it! Just… Get it away," I mutter, standing up while shaking my hand wildly in his general direction.

"Sorry, I should have been mindful of the fact that you're not used to them being this big."

I peek through my fingers enough to see Grayson's face. It's alight with humour, his resplendent eyes dancing. I've never wanted to slap someone as hard!

"You're not funny," I grumble. He takes a step forward, pulling my hands away from my face. I let him because there's no way he can make me look down.

"I want to comment on how amusing you are, Lex, but my shirt on you is very distracting," he says slowly. I'm not sure what should bother me more: the comment on the shirt, or the fact that he shortened my name.

I'm trapped in his gaze. Again. It's like he can pin me down, render me completely useless at any time he pleases, and it's frightfully exciting.

"Almost as distracting as your lack of clothes?" I say, trying to keep my tone borderline sarcastic, but it's as if he's fallen into a predatory world and I'm the focal point.

My hands brace themselves against the bench, clinging to it for dear life. He stands directly in front of me, staring down at me with a gaze so primal, I'm shivering with a sort of unexplainable fear I've never dealt with before.

"Why is it that every time I look at you, I'm distracted?"

"Because you're an idiot. Which is why you're pinning me to this bench," I say, wishing my voice wasn't so shaky.

Grayson smiles wickedly, his face so close to mine that I can feel his warm breath against me. I could push him away right now, but that would mean touching his bare chest.

"Maybe if you weren't so hung up on your assistant, you wouldn't mind."

Is he jealous? Is that why he is always bringing it up? I don't know why he would be.

"Sorry, sometimes I get caught up in..." He glances up at me. "You."

I take a shuddering breath. This isn't going to be an easy mission.

Chapter Eight

The moment I step outside, I am hit in the face with heat. I know I told Grayson I couldn't go out, but this means answers from Jasper. I'm going to have to deal with it.

I aimlessly wander around the side of the main building. If I wasn't concentrating on not fainting from the harsh Sun beating down on me, I might have been admiring all the native trees I've never seen before.

I circle the house four times before giving up. Jasper isn't here. He said outside and I'm here. Yet, he isn't.

Annoyed, I rest my back against the side of the building near a handful of bushes. Without warning, a rustle catches my attention.

"Jasper?" I question as I look through the deep undergrowth. I see dappled light dancing along the forest floor, but shadows still haunt most areas were a possible rabid killer might lurk.

I've seen those horror movies of people wandering into the stupidest of places that any well-minded person would never consider entering, for fear of ending up dead. I decide not to take my chances and I turn around, only to see him right behind me, casually leaning against the wall of the house.

I yelp, nearly collapsing from the heart attack he almost gave me. He only smirks at me, those deep, violet eyes dancing with amusement.

"You scared the hell out of me!" I curse, running a hand through my hair, while the other holds my chest protectively.

"You should be more observant."

"And you shouldn't sneak up on people."

He mindlessly shrugs his shoulders. "I'm used to not being seen."

Taking in a deep breath, I observe him for a moment. He is definitely the man I danced with last night, and who consequently spiked my drink. He is the elusive Alpha creature with the most distinctive eyes.

"Well..."

"What?"

"You're not going to hit me, or yell at me?" He questions, seemingly surprised. He is still leaning against the side of the house.

"It's tempting, but not yet."

Now, he seems more surprised. In the light, I notice how he seems to attract the shadows, as if he is enticing the darkness from the forest with just his presence. It swirls around him, wrapping him in a faint way. I almost pass it off as my imagination.

"So, you don't want to know why I drugged you." He says, so casually. He makes it seem as if everyone does it.

"Would it shock you if I said yes?" I say sardonically.

"Should I just tell you that it worked well in my favor?"

It's my turn to be shocked. *In his favor?* I start to walk away from him.

"Come back here!" He says, as if it is an order.

I turn around and yell, "So, is this what you wanted?"

Jasper smiles gently before pointing his hand in my direction.

"I didn't expect you to fall straight into Grayson's arms, but it did end up working out," Jasper muses, using that smooth gait of his to glide over to a boulder situated underneath a large tree.

"I didn't know he would catch me," I say truthfully. *What would have happened had it been Noah that caught me?*

"No, I wouldn't have allowed that to happen," he says with a smirk.

I flinch, still not used to his strange abilities.

"Speaking of strange abilities, shall I tell you about myself before I tell you why you're here? It might make more sense," he muses.

Jasper doesn't fit into the category of sense. More like the category of contradiction.

"Knock yourself out," I mutter, leaning my back against the trunk of a tree. It feels cool against my skin, which hardly makes sense with the humid air mulling around us.

"Ever heard of the myth of the Phantom Wolves?"

Him being straight to the point knocks the air from my lungs. Phantom Wolves. My worst nightmare.

I close my eyes. "When I was first kidnapped and brought to the Vengeance Pack, my kidnappers used to tell me stories about them so I wouldn't sleep at night."

The memories of those days I wish to forget, but when I try to let go, it's like holding a lighter under my emotions. I can tell Jasper feels my pain by the look he gives me through his dark bangs.

"What is your perception of them?" His voice is like the murmur of the leaves rustling around us.

"Cruel, sadistic, merciless, and evil." I pause, looking up to meet his eyes.

If Jasper is offended by this, he doesn't show it. His fingers tap rhythmically on the rock he sits on.

"You're not completely wrong," he says gently, as if his own words may be hurtful. They aren't. I know it is true, even if the fabrications made by my old Pack members were lies.

"Are you one of them?"

Jasper cringes. "Not just one of them. I am their leader."

I don't doubt it. "Are you all those… things?"

"A Phantom Wolf is cruel only because of his situation. They are created by their own death and sorrow. Myself, on the other hand, I am cursed."

Cursed? I didn't know that was possible. Then again, I didn't believe in Phantom Wolves until now.

"Where do you think Phantom Wolves come from?" He asks, taking me aback for a moment.

"Hell?"

He chuckles. "Think again."

"Magic?"

"And where does magic come from?"

I blink. Then I realize. "The Devotion Pack."

He nods slowly, and I attempt to swallow the lump in my throat. It makes perfect sense for him to be the Alpha of a Pack filled with cursed people, but it still doesn't help me understand why I'm here.

"Gaze Readers, who wield magic to see into people's futures, are the only ones who can naturally become Phantom Wolves," he says in a whisper.

I didn't even know Gaze Readers still existed. Another fable that I'd once doubted.

"Those who control magic, who die with a burden, become trapped souls on earth. However, you can be turned into one. One curse and you're just another Phantom."

Jasper stares at the grass by my feet, and his gaze is clouded over. He looks regretful.

"My father cursed me," he says, voice cracking slightly as he looks up at me. "Only because my own father was scared I would take over his reign of Alpha before he was ready."

My heart pounds and I'm not sure if it's because I'm in the presence of my former nightmare, or in sympathy with this man's tragic life.

"So, I killed him."

My heart stops at the callousness in his words and expression.

"Now, I have a burden on my shoulders. I *can't* die with it, or I'll never become normal again. And I can never be with my mate," he says, and I can't ignore the pain drenching every word coming from his mouth.

"I'm sorry," I say, but the uselessness of my words carries away with the wind.

He stands suddenly and it's as if the nature around us cowers away. It makes sense. It's his burden.

"You think I can help?" I say, unable to cover the doubt in my words with any shred of confidence.

"More than help," he tells me. "You can cure me and everyone else who has been cursed."

He suddenly grabs my hand between his icy fingers, clutching it tight.

"But you can't help me, because you're weak and you're only going to weaken further."

I go to say something, but he cuts me off.

"Only *he* can help stop it," Jasper insists. I shake my head.

"My mate?"

"Yes."

"And who may that be?" I say cynically. Trying to not act slightly interested about who he's about to say. It doesn't make a difference. My mate won't change me. Unless...

"Alpha Grayson."

Chapter Nine

My fist hovers tantalisingly close to the wooden door. If I had any confidence in what I was about to do, I would be knocking, but I don't. I have never had to face something so terrifying in my life. Every ounce of my body is telling me not to do this.

I knock twice on the door.

"Come in," I hear him murmur.

As I turn the knob, my heart is in my throat. Grayson sits behind his desk, pen between his fingers at he writes on a piece of paper. He looks up when I close the door behind me. The most prominent specks of silver glint in his eyes as he catches my gaze.

His office is impressive. More impressive than mine back at home.

"I know," I say, although my voice comes out breathless and hoarse. Grayson's eyebrows furrow together in confusion, not knowing what I am talking about. I force my eyes to the ground.

"Sorry?"

"What... what we are," I tell him, trying to force my voice into sounding somewhat controlled, but instead, it shakes uneasily. Instantly, it clicks with Grayson exactly what I mean.

He sets his pen down, sighing deeply. I watch carefully as he stands, brushing the creases out of his dress shirt before rounding the desk. My heart beats faster as I notice the way his fingers drag across the surface of the desk.

"Who told you?" he questions, leaning against the edge of the desk. At least he is leaving some space between us.

"Someone at the party last night," I say softly. I hope it isn't a mate thing to notice when someone is lying, because otherwise, he would be able to see straight through my façade.

He doesn't seem to notice though, and he frowns in annoyance.

"You weren't supposed to find out this way," he tells me gently, as if it makes a difference. I narrow my eyes at him. "I wanted to be the one to tell you…"

He leans forward, his hand reaching out to me. I take a step back. "Don't."

"Is something wrong?" he asks, surprised at my instant distaste to his touch. I don't want to tell him it is because I'm scared. I take a deep breath, ensuring I am looking directly into Grayson's eyes.

"One man ruined my life," I began. "I wanted to be a lawyer, but one day, my dreams were taken from me. Alpha Kaden stole me from my family when I was only 13. I went from being around some of the most intelligent girls in the world, to the worst criminals in society," I whisper.

I glance down, hating the way Grayson's eyes burn into mine.

"It wasn't the physical torture that bothered me. It was the emotional torment they put me through, night and day. Eventually, when I worked my way to the top, I was forced to betray them."

With a clenched jaw, my gaze sweeps upward again. "That's why I don't trust Alphas.

"When it comes to mates, my sister's mate let four men rape and kill her while she was in heat. It didn't get any better, even when I watched them be euthanized for his crimes." I sigh. "That's why I don't trust mates."

The moment the last word comes from my mouth, Grayson takes a step forward. It shatters the mental wall I spent that entire speech constructing. I knew I felt something with him before. I tried my best not to accept it, but now, as he stands directly in front of me, I can't deny it.

"You have no idea how angry that makes me," he whispers, as if someone else is in the room that might hear. "I would have killed them, every single one of them." He punctuates his words as he places both his hands against the wall. Suddenly, he's so close that I can't breathe.

I want to say something, but the words are stuck in my throat. All I can do is push myself as hard against the wall as possible.

"I want you to trust me," Grayson says, but all I can concentrate on is his hands coming closer to my face.

A rational-minded person would have told him to back up, but it's as if that part of my brain has been closed off. Instead, I'm left eying his fingertips as if they are laced with poison.

Grayson gently brushes his fingers across my cheek. I expect it to be an electric shock straight to my heart, but it is so much more than that. The feeling of the imminent bond between us consumes my entire being, forcing me to accept one simple fact.

We are mates.

He smiles and it's as if he's rejuvenated. I never really noticed how exhausted he usually looks until we touched. He almost seems to light up.

"I would never let anything bad happen to you. Ever." His hot breath invades my senses. Somehow, in the heat of the moment, I believe him.

He places his hand back on the wall, trapping me in. Slowly, as if waiting for me to protest, Grayson brings his head down until I can feel his lips brush against the curve of my neck.

It hits me again. That euphoric feeling only a mate can provide. He gently runs his lips across my neck, completely paralyzing me. The moment those sensuous lips begin leaving soft kisses from below my ear to my collarbone, my knees weaken completely.

"You have no idea how long I've been waiting to do this," Grayson murmurs against my neck, taking advantage of my breathlessness.

My hands, once frozen by my sides, tentatively quiver their way up to his shoulders. My fingers grip his hard muscles. No scraps of teeth against my neck hints he wants to mark me in this situation, which is a relief. Instead, he trails his kisses higher, across my chin with his torturous hands kneading my side.

"Why are you so good at this?" I ask into the air, those being the only words I am able to force out of my mouth. His lips curve into a smile against my skin, making me shiver.

"Shh," he whispers.

All of a sudden, he brings his hands up, pulling away so he can cup my face. I'm trapped in a haze of feeling as he stares deeply into my eyes. I can tell, simply by the look he gives me and the way he tilts his chin slightly, he wants to kiss me.

No, he *is* going to kiss me. When his lips are *so* close to mine, the sound of his office door opening pulls us apart. I am brought back into reality, gasping in air that I hadn't realized I had been holding.

"Oh... Sorry, did I interrupt something?"

Standing in the doorway is a man I've never seen before. His hair is a sun-toned blond and has a similar, shaggy length like Grayson's. He looks mortified that he just walked in on something he wasn't supposed to.

Grayson, on the other hand, looks bothered. He runs a hand through his hair, sighing deeply. I notice at that moment, that the top two buttons of his shirt are unbuttoned. *Did I do that?*

"As a matter of fact, you did," Grayson mutters under his breath.

"Who's this?" The man asks, nodding his head towards me.

I'm still pressed tightly against the wall, remaining stunned by what just happened. I know first-hand how hard it is to resist when someone kisses you like Grayson just did, especially when that someone has a magic touch.

"Lexia, my mate," Grayson informs him. He glances at me. "This is my brother, Evan."

No similarity. That's what I first notice. Maybe the same nose, but other than that, the eye color isn't the same. I would call Evan my relation before Grayson's.

"I came to remind you..." Evan breaks off, casting his gaze over to me. "We have business to attend to."

"Right," Grayson replies, obviously recalling that something important requires his attention.

He looks at me for a fleeting moment, like some sort of a goodbye, before he follows his brother from the room.

I collapse to the ground, completely shattered by what just happened.

Chapter Ten

I lay back on the exquisitely comfortable bed, which I recently claimed as my own. I am becoming accustomed to the fact that this Pack requires not wearing clothes due to the relentless heat. It is hard, but I am seriously considering joining.

As I stare out the open window, the Sun is on a straight course to set behind the horizon.

I am starting to doze off, when a strange skittering sound forces me to open my eyes. I tilt my head downward, and notice the tiniest pebble lying on the floor, its origin of destination unknown. Frowning in confusion, I crawl off the edge of the bed, picking up the strange stone. Am I imagining things, or is Jasper playing with my mind again?

Suddenly, another rock appears, but this time, I catch it as it flies through the window straight toward me. I walk over to the window and duck my head out. A whole floor down, on solid ground, Grayson stands with a decent-sized rock in his hand. Before he notices me, he hurtles it at the window. Instead, it misses, crashing against the side of the wall right by my head.

"Are you crazy?" I yell, having greatly flinched out of the way of the rock. Grayson watches the segments of broken rock tumble back down to the ground.

"I was trying to get your attention," he yells back. I roll my eyes, planting my hands on the windowsill so I won't go tumbling down.

"There would be no attention to be had if you had knocked me unconscious!"

Grayson, despite the situation, lets out a little chuckle as if it's the most entertaining thing he's witnessed. I find myself smiling a little.

"Sorry, I was trying to be romantic," he tells me.

"I suppose you want me to come down there?" I'm not scaling the side of the house, if that's what he's thinking.

Grayson shoves his hands in his pant pockets. "That would be nice."

Sighing, I slam the window shut, but then open it again after realizing how stuffy my room will be when I get back.

Before leaving, I check myself in the mirror. I've never felt this self-conscious and nervous about seeing someone in my life. I'm usually so confident and sure of myself around people. Nevertheless, the way Grayson looks at me strips down every wall I've put up instantly.

When I walk outside, Grayson is leaning casually against the side of the greenhouse holding the stem of a gorgeous yellow flower.

"Good evening," he greets me while holding the flower out towards me. Taking hold of it, I give him a soft smile of appreciation. Someone is trying a little too hard.

Grayson links his arm around mine. "I want to talk to you."

"About?"

He guides me down a narrow dirt path that leads deeper into the garden. He glances down at me as we walk. "Us."

"What about us?" I ask, twisting the stem of the flower between my fingers. "The fact that we are mates?"

As I look around, I wonder who tends to this incredible garden because I can't imagine Grayson with his knees deep in soil. As we enter into the forest, all of the foreign plant life disappears.

"You're okay with it, right?" Grayson asks. I stare at the dappled light from the trees as it flickers across his face.

"I have no choice," I say, giving him a slight smile. "Otherwise, I would be out of here."

He grins, nudging my shoulder playfully. "Very funny."

We walk for a moment in silence and I relish the peacefulness. There wasn't a second of calm in the Vengeance Pack. Always constant rush and noise.

"I get why you're wary about the whole mate thing," Grayson says, kicking a stray pebble on the path. I watch it skitter a little ahead of us, before rolling to a stop.

Suddenly, he stops dead in his tracks, forcing me to as well. He turns and looks down at me, instantly trapping me in his gaze.

"I want you to trust me, and know I'll do anything for you." His voice is so sincere. It's like a mallet breaking into the wall surrounding my heart.

Before I can say a word, he cups my face between his hands, forcing me to keep staring into his eyes. I've never felt this way around a man.

"I will never let anything bad ever happen to you."

"You say it like there is something that I should be worried about," I nervously reply. My assumptions seem true by the painful expression that crosses Grayson's face. I raise an eyebrow.

"I've been getting death threats."

I flinch, my heart jumping at the thought of it. "By who?"

For a moment, Grayson doesn't answer. Instead, he wanders off down the path a little, forcing me to jog to keep up. When I do manage to match his stride, I grab his arm, but he refuses to stop.

"If I knew, they would be six feet under," he tells me and I believe him.

"So, is that why you brought me here?" I question. "To make you stronger so you can find out who is doing this?"

For a Discipline Pack member, it is smart. Your mate makes you stronger, and Grayson needs that if he has any chance against whoever is behind the threats.

"No, that's not it. I brought you here because you are much safer with me," Grayson insists, grabbing my hand in his. There is silence again between us as we trek deeper into the woods.

"There is an uprising," I say suddenly, taking Grayson by surprise. He glances down at me, eyebrow raised as if he expects me not to know anything about it.

"I don't know the full scale of it, but I do know someone who is involved," I admit. One betraying son of a bitch.

Grayson tightens his grip on my hand while he waits for me to continue talking.

I sigh. "His name is Reilly. He was my partner for a long time. What I didn't know, was that he was secretly working to get me to lead an uprising against all the Packs. I wanted an uprising, but mainly against Kaden. Instead, I was fuelling something greater, and I hate myself for it..."

Grayson stops. I pause, wanting to listen more to the sound of the soft breeze blowing through the leaves, rather than his scolding voice, but his answer surprises me.

"We need to find him then. If we do, then we could have a complete monopoly over this!"

I have my doubts, though. "But who knows where he could be? Any Pack could be hiding him."

My spiteful words make Grayson laugh, despite the impending political issue.

"We will find him, and when we do..."

Suddenly, Grayson's voice drifts off. I stare at him, noticing the way he looks over me completely, as if something beyond the trees has stolen his attention.

"The Sun is setting," he whispers.

"Is everything okay?" I ask him warily, noticing a look of fright in his eyes that suddenly casts a shadow over his beautiful features.

His jaw clenches. "You need to get back home."

"Then let's just walk back," I say. As I go to turn around, I catch him shaking his head. He backs up a few steps, taking me by surprise. I have never seen such a sudden change in his persona like this before.

"You follow the path home. I have something to do."

Without another word, completely ignoring my protests, he disappears into the forest. The darkness almost seems to swallow him whole.

What the hell was that? All of a sudden, it was as if I was facing a completely different person, not my mate and the Alpha of Freedom. Shaking my head in disbelief, I decide to just head back to the house, and question him about it tomorrow.

"You're looking good, Lexia."

The sudden, very familiar voice from behind me makes me jump. Twisting around, I come to see a person standing in the middle of the path, looking sadistically happy with his findings.

It is Reilly. I nearly collapse on the spot.

"What are you doing here?" I growl. With the Sun now only moments away from concealing itself beneath the treeline, darkness and shadows are spreading around us.

"I came to see you," he tells me. His deep, blue eyes glint in the rising moonlight.

"Well, I'm not interested in talking to you," I mutter as I try to walk past him. "Not since you betrayed me."

Reilly grabs my arm tightly, stopping me from walking away. Instantly, my heart begins to beat a little faster. I wouldn't be scared of him if I hadn't been tricked and manipulated by him in the past.

"I didn't betray you. You wanted an uprising and I fuelled it." I rip away from him, stumbling back a few steps.

"Not a complete rebellion against the Packs! I wanted to show Kaden what it's like to have your life taken from you, not this," I tell him.

Reilly narrowed his eyes at me. "You're only saying this because you're with an Alpha now. Hypocrite."

The audacity of him. *Who does he think he is?* He is losing it. He doesn't understand the position I am in, and I doubt he ever will.

"Don't you dare call me that! You are the one who thinks they can create an army big enough to take over these Packs. You're out of your mind," I snap, making Reilly's face darken in anger.

"You have no idea what is planned, but you will soon," he says.

I don't know what he means, until a bag is shoved over my head from behind. Then everything goes black.

Chapter Eleven

Grayson

"When did Lexia go missing?"

Resting my elbows on my desk, I look directly at Detective Simone sitting in front of me. She is dressed immaculately while clutching a pad of paper; a detective from the Discipline Pack who is anxious to find out where my mate has vanished.

She looks painfully like Lexia too. Despite a different facial structure, and her square-rimmed glasses, she has the same green eyes and slightly off-color blonde hair.

"I don't know. Six days, maybe?" I can't remember because every moment has me on edge. I have never felt this much pain in my life.

"Four days, actually."

I glance to over at Landon, Alpha of Power. His deep, brown eyes stare at me worryingly. He has been a good friend of mine for some time. When he found out Lexia went missing, he offered to leave his mate and new-born daughter for a few days to assist me.

"What do you think happened to her?" Simone asks, tucking a blonde piece of hair behind her ear. Maybe it was stupid of me to hire someone who looks so much like Lexia, but all the best detectives are from the Discipline Pack.

Landon places his hand on the edge of the desk, getting my attention. "Let's be realistic."

"Yeah, realistic..."

I glance over to Simone's right at the Alpha of Love. He lounges back on his chair while folding a piece of paper. Another willing friend of mine. Little did I know that Landon and Malik did not have the best relationship.

"And by realistic, we mean, *not* Malik's idea," Landon states, refusing to look at Malik, who sits up, openly offended.

"Realistically, I believe Lexia was kidnapped," I tell Simone. She writes down the information on her little pad of paper.

The words hurt to say. They burn at my throat and my body doesn't want to admit that maybe it was a possibility. I don't have much time to think about it though, as Malik cuts in.

"That was my idea," he tells Simone, glancing over to her paper. "Did you get that down? That was *my* idea."

Landon and I collectively roll our eyes.

"So, we seem to have the same opinion?" Simone decides, sizing up both Alphas beside her. I feel bad for putting her between the two brooding men, but I would rather not have a fight break out in my office.

"No. I think that she left him, it's that simple. What woman in her right mind would let a man bring her here against her will, and propose she has no other option than to stay? I would have left..." Landon declares.

The truth in Landon's words hurts. Maybe I shouldn't have told Landon everything.

Malik coughs. "As the Alpha..."

"Here we go," Landon mutters.

"... of Love, I must say that *that* is the stupidest thing I've heard."

"You're the stupidest thing," Landon mumbles under his breath.

Malik sits up on his seat, twisting so he can look over at Landon. "Say that to my face, I dare you!"

"Obviously, we have differences here, but can we resolve these once we have found Lexia?" I snap in annoyance. Malik slumps back in his seat, defeated.

Simone breathes in deeply, collecting herself.

"So, if she has been kidnapped..."

Landon scoffs. I narrow my eyes at him in warning, much to Malik's enjoyment.

"We need to find out who did it," Simone proposes. A sliver of optimism crawls its way through the bleakness that has been the past few days. If I find Lexia, I will never let her go. Well, at least never let her outside, at night, alone.

"Well, if she has been taken, we need to send armies out to find her, *now*," Landon says. Tactical, as always.

Malik chuckles. "Oh yes, the Alpha of Power has to let his armies do something, considering they are useless back in his Pack."

I sigh deeply, knowing Malik's mocking words have pressed at a part of Landon that I know he doesn't appreciate.

"Well, at least my Pack isn't full of sappy idiots whose only life goal is to find their mate."

"At least they stay with their mates."

"What would you know about mates?"

"Ah... Alpha of Love, right here."

"Ironic how the Alpha of Love can't find his mate..."

"Neither can you."

"At least I can keep a relationship."

"Hey, my relationships last the night."

"Also, isn't it ironic how the Alpha of Love has sex with..."

"Just sharing my love around!"

Simone takes us all by surprise, as she suddenly swings her pad of paper to smack Malik straight in the face. Then Landon right after. I smother my smile behind my hand as Malik rubs the side of his head and Landon huffs.

"Lexia is out there, possibly being held hostage, and you two are here arguing about this?" Simone says, sounding exasperated. I don't blame her. Every moment sitting here, thinking about Lexia's fate, is frightening.

"Okay, if we are going to try finding her, I think we should start in the Vengeance Pack where she was originally from," Landon says.

Malik goes to interrupt, but I glare straight into his glassy, blue eyes attempting to warn him.

"I like that idea," I muse. Maybe, with a twist of Mara's finger, we can get Kaden to help us out in finding her. I just need her back here with me.

Glancing at Malik, I notice the Alpha of Love looking very thoughtful.

"I think we should get a Gaze Reader. Maybe they can see what happened to Lexia," Malik says. Everyone pauses, as the first words of reason for the day come out of his mouth. Of course. A Gaze Reader could look into my eyes and find Lexia.

***

My personal Gaze Reader, Esmeralda, wanders into the room. A brightly-colored shawl covers half her face. She came from the Devotion Pack after ideas of Phantom Wolves scared the majority of the Pack members out. I let her stay on the condition that she would serve me when I needed her to. Ever since, she has predicted a lot of my life.

Unfortunately, she walks in on two idiots arguing.

"My ancestors created the word *soul mate*," Malik says.

"Wish they didn't create *you*," Landon retorts.

"Esmeralda! Great to see you," I say, cutting Landon and Malik's voices off.

Slowly, she unwraps the fabric around her head. "I can sense the tension in the room. I hope I can find Lexia."

It doesn't surprise me that she knows without having to be told. Without a word, she leans over my desk, eyes latched to mine. It's not hard to keep eye contact when she draws you, as if she has puppet strings attached to your limbs. I can feel her searching, looking into the future for clues. The feeling is strange, as if someone is violating my privacy, but I sit still through the intrusion.

"She is saved in the future."

I nearly collapse in relief. If we find her, she'll be safe.

"But I can't see who by. I see a shadowy figure, swooping in when needed most," she says, voice drawn and heavy as she falls into the trance that is my future. She can't delve too deep without seriously injuring herself, but she can still scrape at the surface.

"But she is saved and returned here," she tells us. I want to sigh in relief, but the thought of the shadowy figure saving her has me worried.

"We should head out to look for her then. *Now.*"

Chapter Twelve

Lexia

I don't know how long I've been tied here. I'm dehydrated, hungry, and extremely tired. The real torture is coming from this state between sleep and consciousness. I am constantly fighting against the haze that surrounds me and it is exhausting.

I began counting the days by the amount of times one man visited. He would take advantage of my weakness and drug me, so the nights and mornings would slip by.

This time when the door opens, Reilly walks in. I also expect him to drug me so he can keep me here even longer.

"Pig," I mutter, salvaging enough of my hoarse voice. He smiles crookedly, strolling casually with someone in tow.

"Delightful as ever," he muses, kicking the door closed behind him.

Escaping might have been a possibility. The rope around my wrist seems to have loosened over the course of the past few days, but the drugs render my limbs useless.

"There are two things I hate about you," I mutter, looking up at him through the curtain of hair sticking to my face. He raises an eyebrow in amusement.

"Your face. Now shut both of them!"

He grins. "I don't think you're in the situation to be saying those things to me." He stands directly in front of me, looking down as I sit in the chair.

"Why am I here? If you think for a second I'll help you with this uprising, you better forget it," I growl.

He stoops down, bringing himself to my level. My vision slightly spins, making me contemplate whether I might end up throwing up all over him. Just the look on his face makes me nauseous.

"Obviously, you don't have much of a choice. Tell me what you know of the uprising…"

"As much as you do. We worked together, Reilly, and you lied! I'm no help to you, so let me go," I beg, my voice a pleading mess. I want nothing more than to get out of here.

Is Grayson looking for me? Does he even care?

"I can't. They all know. Your Pack knows. Other Packs know. They know you're leading this thing, and they won't stop until they win," he tells me. I jump as he rests his hand on my knee.

"I'm not leading anything! I wanted to take down Kaden, but I don't want *every* Alpha taken down," I say, shaking my leg back and forth so his hand will fall off.

Reilly's hand slides further up my thigh, despite how pressed together they are.

"You may not know anything, but you're going to help me," he murmurs, leaning further over me. "In more ways than one."

I swing my head forward, smacking him in the head. Not expecting my retaliation, he stumbles backward. Much to my pleasure and despite the instant splitting headache that begins to form, it's better than Reilly's hand crawling on me.

"Why don't you just kill me instead? That would be better than working with you!"

"I'm not the one behind all this, Lexia. One man wants you, and he will get you," Reilly says.

Suddenly, his persona has changed, becoming sullen, stern, and serious. The mention of this 'man' must have both of our hearts skipping a beat.

"A man? Who?" I find myself asking.

I don't have to hear his name, but by the agitation on his face, I can tell that he is nothing but frightening.

"Let's hope you never have to find out. Accept my offer to help me, and you won't get hurt. Neither will Grayson," he tells me.

My hearts stops at the mention of my mate. Would he, or whoever is behind this mess, hurt him? If those death threats were followed through, then I would never forgive myself. Especially, since it was my stupid idea to start that uprising.

"Please don't hurt him…"

"We won't have to. The uprising you started has gotten a lot of attention already. All I need you to do is restart the fire in the Vengeance Pack…"

All of a sudden, Reilly is cut off as something whizzes past and hits the wall behind us. Twisting as far as my tied, weak body will let me, I see a bronze-stemmed arrow sunk deeply into the wall.

As I turn back around, my eyes meet a shadowed figure in the doorway. Whoever is able to get in without either Reilly or I hearing, is a mystery to me. The silhouette of a bow can be seen as he steps forward.

In one swift movement, the stranger loads the bow and points it directly at the man Reilly first brought in with him. As he begins to walk forward, the sliver of sunlight from the small, barred window reveals his identity. However, he is not someone I have ever seen before.

Dressed as if he's about to commit some vulgar crime, the stranger expresses no emotion, which instils me with fear. His facial features make him look young. However, they are also etched with maturity and experience.

He stares directly at me and something sparks within his warm irises, a lighter brown than anything that I have ever seen before. His eyes match beautifully with his hair, and for a fleeting moment in time, I consider the fact that, despite this attraction, there's something dark about him.

"Cal," Reilly growls.

They know each other. Cal's jaw clenches tightly. Whatever past relationship they have, it can't be very good.

"Didn't think we would have to see each other again," the man muses. Instantly, I'm faced with an accent I've never heard in my life. It's so exotic, the way it melts smoothly together, curving around the senses.

"And in such an unfortunate place," Reilly muses.

I glance between Cal and Reilly. Both glare directly at each other, waiting for the other to waver.

"You know why I'm here," Cal says smoothly, motioning to me with his forehead. If I wasn't so stunned, then maybe I would have said something snarky in reply. Instead, I sit on this chair, mouth hanging open slightly.

"And you know why I can't let you take her."

Cal smirks a little. The act lights his entire face up, even though I see it's more out of spite. As I look at him, I'm torn. *Does Cal want to help me escape, or is there another reason?*

"Get me out of here," I say, using the strength in my voice to my favor. It doesn't matter anyway, because both men ignore me.

"How many strings did your boss have to pull to get you here? Huntsman."

The words Reilly say are so snake-like and evil. Hatred drips from the sentence, especially when he says Huntsman. When I look at Cal, it makes sense for him to be one of the strong Wolves hired by Alphas to hunt down specific individuals.

Did Grayson send him?

"How much I am paid is none of your business. Now, you can either hand the girl over, or I shoot you in the heart," Cal says.

Obviously, Reilly feels the weight of the threat. With no way to protect himself, Reilly has nothing to do but obey.

"And piss *him* off?"

There it is again. Him. Who is this man no one is telling me about?

"I have a job. Hand her over," Cal says sternly, unmoving from his objective.

I try moving my arms enough to free myself from the rope, but I am too weak. At least I've gained control over them again. Maybe I can slink out of here in the shadows.

"And if *he* comes for her?" Reilly asks. Cal sighs deeply, strolling forward a few steps. I know he sees me pulling at the thick rope, trying to loosen it around my wrists. His gaze is as sharp as his wit.

"It is not my job to care…" Cal mutters. Waiting for Reilly to say something else, the Huntsman loads up his bow, mainly as a threat. The moment Cal aims towards Reilly, he is quick to raise his hands up in defeat. "Take her then and watch your work be in vain!"

At that exact moment, the rope around my wrists finally gives way and I fall to the floor. I stumble to my feet, but my legs wobble and sway.

Without a word, Cal swiftly sends an arrow into Reilly's thigh, causing him to topple to the ground. Positioning the bow away from me, Cal holds out his hand.

"I'm going to take you back to Grayson," he tells me, obviously noticing my hesitation to take his hand.

At the mention of Grayson, I can't help but take his hand. He rescued me.

I was being kept underground, and as he pushes me through the hatch and onto the forest floor of the Freedom Pack, I almost scream with joy.

Perhaps if my limbs had been working well, I would have danced and thrown leaves into the air.

"Why did you do that?" I question Cal, as he clambers out after me and kicks the trap door closed. He turns to look at me. In the light, he is so much more handsome, but something painful and deep lies within his gaze.

"It's my job. What my boss says goes."

"Who's your boss? Grayson?"

When he shakes his head, his light-brown hair presses against his forehead. "Look, we need to get you back home," Cal says, glancing at the Sun. My eyes stay on the Huntsman, knowing my eyes would burn if I looked at the sky, after being locked up for so many days.

"What Pack are you from? Your accent isn't familiar," I note, causing him to chuckle.

"These little things you want to know are useless. I hope we never have to meet again," Cal tells me seriously. I narrow my eyes at him.

"It's my job and I hope you aren't in that position again," he explains before I can get offended.

"When you get back to Grayson, I want you to tell him you escaped. There is no need for him to be interested in my presence," Cal orders.

He wants me to lie to Grayson?

"But I'm weak, I'm hardly walking on my own," I point out. It's true. My arm clutches Cal's as we walk, trying to keep my feet from slipping out from under me.

"You're stronger than you think. He won't doubt it."

We walk for a while in silence. My mind is trying to gather that some man who doesn't know me was sent by someone from another Pack to save me. I'm struggling though.

"Does this mean I owe you?" I ask meekly, glancing sideways at Cal.

He stares down at me, eyes glinting from the Sun. "No. Consider it my parting gift to you."

Right. Never to see each other again. Suddenly we stop. "Here is where I say goodbye. Grayson will smell me if I get any closer."

After a few mild directions, I am confident I will make it back.

"Thank you. I probably would have died had you not saved me."

He picks up my hand and brings it to his lips, kissing it softly. The gesture is bittersweet, as he backs away a few steps.

"Go home, Lexia. Your mate is waiting."

Chapter Thirteen

Malik stands before me, staring at me as if he doesn't believe I truly exist.

Cal, the Huntsman, abandoned me not far back from Grayson's home. My journey back was only a short walk. Except, I had expected to see Grayson when I first opened the front door. I am rather surprised when the Alpha of Love faces me.

"Lexia?"

"Malik," I reply, tilting my head.

I fold my arms over my chest, wishing he would move out of the way. The setting Sun beats on my back, and a glass of water sounds very good right now. I also want to see Grayson.

"How did you…Where were you?" He questions me, still not budging from his position. I sigh, running my hand through my hair.

"Can I see Grayson, please?"

Malik looks stunned for a moment. "Right. Ah, he's in the Vengeance Pack right now. I'll let him know you're back."

I follow Malik inside, who is still asking me relentless questions about where I've been the past week. Honestly, all I want to do is collapse my weak body into a bed, but I supply Malik with the basics of my kidnapping.

I leave out the details of the strange Huntsman named Cal from an unknown Pack. He had told me to keep a secret, and at this time, I'm not jumping on the idea of selling him out. I mean, he's proved how good he is with a bow and arrow.

"That's impressive how you managed to escape," he points out.

"I know, right," I mutter under my breath.

After providing him with some explanation, Malik manages to leave me alone for a while. I think he gets the hint that his job is over from the nurse I see to check if the drugs I've been given aren't too dangerous to my system. Luckily, she prescribes me food, water, and sleep. I am left to crawl into the comfortable bed and wait for Grayson.

I could have slept, lying there in the clutches of pure softness and silk, but every time I close my eyes, Grayson is there, and Cal, and Reilly, and even Jasper.

Where is that elusive Alpha of Devotion, anyway?

Okay, maybe I can't sleep.

Instead, I just lie in bed, fingers tapping against my arms as I keep them folded across my stomach. As I stare at the ceiling, alone in the darkness, I wonder how long it will be before my Alpha returns home.

***

When I awaken, the Sun still hasn't set, which leads me to believe I didn't sleep for long. Sighing, I roll over, only to be faced with a pair of silver eyes staring down at me.

I feel my heart completely stop beating at that moment.

At the same time as I look at my mate, it is as if I am in the presence of another man. His expression mirrors my own. He is weak, distraught, and tired. He has dark shadows under his eyes, and his face is gaunt with worry.

"I thought I had lost you," he murmurs, his voice cracking ever so slightly.

I sit up in the bed, throwing my arms around his broad shoulders, pushing him closer to me. This last week has been hell, and the feeling of Grayson in my arms is my only solace.

"I'm so sorry," he whispers in my ear as his hands run repeatedly down my back. I can hear the angst and honesty in his voice as he repeats the words 'I'm sorry' over again.

My own words burn in my throat. "It wasn't your fault."

65

He pulls my head down to his chest, and I can hear the erratic beating of his heart. He's been beating himself up over this, I can tell. If Reilly hadn't have kidnapped me then, he would have found another way. I want to express the words, but my emotions are forcing them down.

Grayson pulls away, holding my shoulders back so he can look at me. Reilly never hit me once. No one did. That was not part of Reilly's intentions. I could tell that Grayson is relieved to see no marks on me.

"What happened? Why? Who do I have to kill?"

His questions come at me like wild fire, and I have to take a moment to assess what to tell him.

"A man I used to work with. His name is Reilly. He wanted me to be a part of his stupid uprising."

Grayson's face immediately darkens.

"I managed to escape. He was keeping me in some sort of underground holding place. I'm sure if I agreed to his plan…"

Grayson stands up in a second, leaving the spot where he was sitting vacant and cold. I catch his blazing silver eyes, overflowing with livid emotions and excitement.

"I'll alert someone. We will find this place and destroy it."

He turns his back from me and, for a fleeting moment, I am scared he's going to leave me. He is so caught up in his anger towards himself, that he's about to leave me alone in this bed to fight for vengeance.

"Grayson… wait!" I call out, just as his hand reaches for the door handle. I'm not about to let that man walk out that door, and I know he can hear it in my strained voice.

He turns slowly, meeting my gaze again.

"You're not seriously leaving me here?"

Instantly, I see a flood of understanding overcome him. He knows what I am insinuating without me having to say a single word. In a brief moment, his expression changes from the angry, spiteful young Alpha, to a man who understands my fear.

He walks back to the bed, determined as ever. Close enough to touch, Grayson stoops down, bracing his arms on either side of my body. For the first time, I don't mind in the slightest.

"I'll never leave you," he whispers. His face and lips are so close to mine. I can feel his body against me as he kneels upon the bed, consuming me with the feeling only a mate can inflict.

Reaching my hands up, I cup both sides of his face, feeling the softness of his skin. Everything about him, in this moment seems so perfect.

"Kiss me."

His lips touch mine and the feeling is like no other. It can't get any better than this... but it can. Grayson's hands slowly glide down the side of my ribcage to my waist, which he holds like the most fragile thing in existence. Even my hands have an insatiable need as they thread through the thickness of Grayson's hair, pulling it as if I can't get enough.

The taste of him, against my lips, is so sweet.

Grayson gently pulls away.

I stare up at him, the reflection in his eyes showing the redness of my cheeks. Then he smiles, the juvenile Alpha I know is back. "I told you, you'd have to beg for more."

I scrunch my nose up in disagreement, remembering his spoken promise that time in the kitchen. At the time, I fully despised the idea of being with him in anyway, but now, my body yearns for it.

I watch him glance at the window and for a moment, I think he's admiring the sunset. Then he crawls off me.

"And I can't wait to hear it," he tells me with a crooked smirk on his face. I narrow my eyes, wanting to retort back with the fact that me begging will never happen, but the words stay within my mind.

I catch his wink as he departs from the room, before I slide out of bed. Twice he's done this now, and I want to find out why.

I'm going to follow him.

Chapter Fourteen

I pad down the stairs, warily keeping my eyes on Grayson. I feel bad for following him, but I don't know what else to do. It's something about the sunset that gets him on edge, and I don't think the curious side of me is going to let it go until I find out why.

He walks quickly, looking around as if he's searching for someone. He doesn't seem to find who he's looking for, and his face transforms into fear. He leads me towards the front door without even knowing it.

I keep a fair distance once we make it outside. I keep behind trees, my footsteps light, as he strolls into the forest with determination.

Where is he going?

I pause, pressing my hand against a tree as I look around. I catch Grayson pushing through the undergrowth as if it's nothing. My heart flutters with the excitement of following him. If he catches me, I might be in big trouble, but I'm too anxious to turn around now.

I continue to follow him, skipping from tree to tree while Grayson moves quickly ahead. His long strides force us deeper into the forest. As he walks, he manages to pull his shirt off, tossing it off to the side.

The sun, almost completely behind the horizon, illuminates the muscles of his back as he moves. It beckons me as the dim light crawls deeper through the trees, infecting every little space with darkness.

The idea comes unpleasantly into my mind that he's meeting some girl, and I try to brush away the thought. Grayson isn't like that.

Suddenly, he stops in his tracks, just as I am about to hop to the next tree trunk. I slide backward, concealing myself as he turns his head slightly. I'm far enough back that he can't have heard my footsteps, but something has caught his attention.

Then, he starts walking again. His hands are shoved into his pant pockets, and he's facing the disappearing Sun.

Before I can make it any further, a hand covers my mouth.

"Are you out of your mind?" A familiar voice says into my ear.

I kick and pull, pushing myself from his grip. Twisting around, I meet the alert, violet eyes that belong to only one Alpha in this world. Jasper.

"Were you following me?" I question angrily, brushing out my clothes that he just wrinkled. He raises a dark eyebrow from beneath his ruffled hair.

"Returning the favor on behalf of Grayson," he muses, leaning back against the tree. Glancing over my shoulder, I notice Grayson has continued off into the forest, completely oblivious to Jasper and I.

"Why are you here?"

He shrugs. "I'm everywhere."

Sighing, I run a hand through my hair. Now that I've stopped walking, the cold is seeping through my clothes and attacking my skin.

"Is there a particular reason why you stopped me?"

Again, he shrugs. "It's getting dark."

"That's it? It's dark, so you're suggesting I go back?"

He smiles weakly and nods. Somehow, it's as if I can see behind his eyes, and I notice he's lying. He's not just here because it's dark. Sure, it's probably part of the reason, but be doesn't want me following Grayson by any means.

"You were just kidnapped after doing something stupid like this," He smartly reminds me.

"I was left behind after Grayson did exactly this."

He cocks his head. "He just waltzed off into the forest as if it's nothing."

Jasper shakes his head. "He didn't ask you to follow him."

I hate the banter Jasper and I share. He's mostly right, and when he isn't, he makes it seem like arguing with him is pointless.

All of a sudden, a cruel, detached howl fills the air. Jasper and I both freeze, the blood draining from my face.

"We need to go," Jasper insists and grabs my wrists. I snatch them away.

"What was that?" I question. "That wasn't Grayson, was it?"

Jasper, glancing around, assesses the shadows sliding in between the trees as the Sun finally sets. His ring glints in the rising moonlight. *Commander of the Night.*

"Be quiet," He snaps. I fold my arms against my chest, forcing his hand to fall back to his side.

"I'm not doing anything until you tell me what's going on. Do you know how isolating it…"

I yelp as Jasper casually bends down, wrapping his arms around my waist as he throws me face-first over his shoulder.

"Let me go!" I growl, my hands slapping hard against his back. He chuckles, despite being almost terrified moments before. Ignoring my protests, he turns on his heels and begins walking back the way we came.

"Nothing is going on. It's a full Moon tonight. Maybe some Goddess worshippers are out," Jasper muses. I don't stop slamming my fists against his back.

The Moon is full tonight, but I still don't see much. I just want off Jasper's back.

"I'd rather be kidnapped," I mutter. "Speaking of, thanks for helping me."

My words come out half-jokingly, with a slight roll of the eyes, but a part of me means it. He didn't bother to come find me, after proclaiming his desire to protect and help me.

"I was waiting for Grayson to do something. You don't know the mental torment I endured having to watch him wander around other Packs like a chicken without a head."

The image in my head makes me smile a little.

"So you know about the uprising he offered me to take part in?" I don't know how we managed to get off the topic of Grayson, or the fact I'm still on his back. Irritatingly, he's *that* distracting.

"Indeed. Now I must admit, that kid did a good job of rescuing you," he tells me.

"Cal? He's not *that* young, is he?"

Jasper chuckles. "Everyone's young to me."

Suddenly, he sets me down. Stretching, I look through the trees. I can see the lights of Grayson's house close by.

"Even Kaden?"

This time, Jasper laughs aloud. "Kaden's great, great…"

He pauses, "… great, great grandparents didn't even exist when I killed my father."

Startled, I look up to meet his gaze.

"Remember, I'm not really alive."

He grabs my hand, and I jump. His skin is ice-cold, like a Phantom. It doesn't feel right, and neither does his heart when he places my palm across his chest. No heartbeat. Nothing.

"That's why I need you," he murmurs, voice suddenly low and serious. The scrutiny in his gaze is unnerving. "It can't be beaten without your help."

"Why me?"

His jaw clenches as he lets my hand fall back down to my side. "I need you to kill someone for me."

I flinch. *Kill?* Like all those criminals back in the Vengeance Pack, I swore I would never become one of them. I feel as if I'm going to throw up. I can tell that Jasper is being completely serious.

"My father wasn't the one to curse me. He asked one man to do it. If he dies, my soul will be replenished, and I can be with my mate," Jasper sounds desperate.

My mind spins. "Why can't you kill him?"

"That will only worsen my burden. I need to help someone to end this, and it's going to help you!"

71

"How is murder going to help me?" I ask him. Nothing he's saying is making much sense.

He grabs his hair, clearly frustrated by what he has to explain. He even begins to pace, feet crunching across fallen leaves on the ground.

"This man…" He paused. "He kidnapped you."

"Reil…"

"No. No, this man is worse than him…"

My face twists in confusion, and then it clicks. *The man.* The one Cal and Reilly mentioned, but never told me anything about. The one man who truly needs me for the uprising.

One man wants you, and he will get you.

Taunting words ring painfully in my head. "Who is he?"

"A Phantom. He's as old as I, and after being betrayed by the Alpha of Wisdom, he wants nothing but the Pack system to fail."

"Sounds familiar," I murmur, hating myself.

"Sure, you wanted the collapse of the Pack system too, but he wants to force everyone to live under his command. He's a sick man, Lexia. As much as I would like to keep you from him, it's necessary you end his life."

The information unfurls in my brain, as I try process what he means. I kill and the results are that Jasper becomes a part of the living and finds his mate. It will also end this uprising once and for all.

Jasper grabs my hand, making me sit down on a boulder while he paces in front of me.

"But… But you're too weak…"

"This again."

"You can't kill a Phantom on your own. You need to be marked," Jasper explains, as if it's something I would commit to every day. My hand unconsciously reaches for my neck. A mark would brand me as an Alpha's property for the rest of my life.

Jasper grabs my shoulders, shaking me slightly.

"I know you're feeling the mate bond," Jasper points out. I narrow my eyes at him, shrugging his hands off me. He's right. Completely right.

"I'll try, okay," I tell him, clambering to my feet. "But I'm not going to bare my neck to him like a Love Pack member."

He backs off a little, chuckling at my joke. I doubt he thinks much of Alpha Malik.

"I get it. I suppose you'll want something in return," Jasper muses, giving me a wink that has me instantly knowing what he's insinuating. Wanting Grayson and I to be together is one thing, but this...

"I'm not discussing my sex life with you," I tell him, furrowing my brows. He laughs, and I admire for a moment how musical his voice really is.

I have no doubt his mate will adore him.

"Don't say it like I don't have experience," he jokes, nudging my side with his elbow.

"I didn't need to know that," I say honestly. "Shall we go back to the house? It's cold out here."

Chapter Fifteen

I lie in bed with my hands folded over my stomach. It's late, but I can't bring myself to sleep. Jasper may have explained what that howl was, but I can't get the eerie sound out of my head. It curls around my mind, ringing in my ears. That wasn't a prayer to the Moon Goddess. It was something darker and more sinister.

Unable to find sleep for the second time today, I make the decision to get up and wander around. The night is balmy and thick, so being naked under the sheet I wrap around myself is a mild relief.

The rooms of the house are large and open, with the windows wide to let in cool air. It dances across my bare skin, relieving the feeling of pent-up heat under my skin. No one is around, and I couldn't be happier.

Wherever Grayson is right now, I don't care. I walk up a flight of stairs, sheet dragging at my ankles. I would be beyond embarrassed if someone was to show up right now and see me dressed like this.

The moment I make it upstairs, the entire layout of the place seems to change. My feet remain on the edge of the step as I wonder whether I should go any further. It's darker up here and less open.

Something suggests that I shouldn't be up here. I should turn around, but right at the end of the hallway, there is an oak door calling for me. No. I will ask him about it first before entering.

I twist on my feet, deciding I should not be snooping around, until I hear a faint creak.

I close my eyes and take a deep breath. My curiosity is intrigued by the sound. Slowly, I turn around, like a girl in a horror movie about to face a monster. Instead, I see the door. Except this time, it's slightly open.

"Was that a sign, Goddess?" I ask into the air. "I'll just glance in," I decide, padding across the carpet on my tiptoes. I try to talk myself out of it, but my mind suggests otherwise.

Pressing my hand against the surface of the door, cursing my curiosity, I push it wide open.

For a moment, I don't know what I am looking at. At first, I believe that I have just set foot into some crime scene investigation room. As I turn around to survey the room, I am caught off guard by a six-foot tall picture of a menacing wolf. I gasp in terror before realizing the picture isn't real.

The rest of the walls have pictures of the exact same wolf scattered around, covering the decorative wallpaper. The pictures are accompanied with ripped-out pages from books with some words underlined with bright red marker.

My mind spins as I attempt to make sense of what I am seeing. Why in the world does Grayson have a room dedicated primarily to an unknown wolf? The thought makes me shiver.

Tentatively, I wander into the room a little further. Up close, I can see the dead soul in the creature's eyes. Someone had to have been close enough to take a photo of this beast, and I can't imagine anyone that would be brave enough to do so. Unless Grayson is the culprit. I mean, this is his room...

My fingers brush against the paper pinned to the wall, vandalized by ugly crosses, question marks, and unexplained lines. Looking a little closer, I can see, with horror, that these pages are about Phantom Wolves.

The stories I was told as a child, and was scared of, are being displayed right in front of my eyes. Words such as cursed, mate, and Phantom Wolf are circled all over the pages. Swallowing, I walk across the room. Nothing is adding up. None of the information is anything I would have expected to see in here.

"What are you hiding from me, Grayson?" I ask, slightly glad he isn't here to answer.

He must know. He *has* to. You don't just have articles on Phantom Wolves hanging on your wall as an art form. Grayson wants to know something, and by the giant red question mark drawn crudely across the left wall, he hasn't found it out yet.

Unless…

I notice something glint underneath the question mark that I haven't noticed before. It is only a small photo, but a massive red circle around it draws my eyes closer.

Plucking the photo from its spot, I see what it truly signifies. Me. It is a picture of my face. An old picture, but it is definitely me.

Suddenly, as I stare into my own glossed eyes, I realize I am tied to whatever this mess is. In addition, Grayson knows about it.

My heart races as the photograph slips from my fingers, fluttering to the ground by my feet.

What does he want with me?

Suddenly, the sound of someone clearing their throat alerts me of their presence. Whirling around, I'm caught in the gaze of Grayson and he doesn't look very happy.

Actually, he doesn't even look sane.

Chapter Sixteen

I can't breathe. The man who meets my gaze is almost in a trance. Soulless, but so alive.

"I can explain…" I say, before I know what is coming out of my mouth. A blush has crept so deeply onto my face, I'm almost positive my cheeks are stained forever. Standing under his scrutinizing gaze, I've never felt so embarrassed in my life.

I expect his expression to contort in anger. I have snuck into something obviously meant to be private, or at the very least, kept a secret.

"Entertain me," he murmurs, his voice taunting and sly.

I assume he means he wants an explanation. How mad will he be if I tell him my curiosity is what forced me into this room? I can't imagine what the repercussions will be.

"I was exploring, but I didn't mean to come across this room."

A wicked smile is etched into his features. "Do you like what you see?" He asks, motioning to what is pinned behind me. Glancing over my shoulder, my eyes meet the darkened ones of that wolf.

I shake my head. "It looks like it would kill me if it could."

Grayson raises his eyebrows, seeming somewhat normal for a brief second.

"Oh, he would never kill you," he tells me, his words bland, but something in his eyes suggests he means it.

By his tone, he knows this wolf well. Well enough to know whom it would kill, and whom it wouldn't.

"Where were you tonight?"

He takes a step forward, so graceful and calculated. At the same time, it comes off as predatory. My back is close to the wall and my hands are clutching the top of the sheet wrapped around my body.

"Do you want me to keep going?" He asks, reminding me of what I have wanted for that one moment in time. I can still feel his hands on my body, and the taste of his lips on mine.

He takes another step forward.

"I just want to know what you were doing," I press, wondering if I will regret it.

Grayson sighs. "And I want to know how far you would have followed me…"

Shit.

"I… I can't apologize for wanting to know what my mate is doing," I explain.

Almost amused, Grayson begins a gentle walk back and forth in front of me. I watch his every move, waiting for a change in his behavior. He's being so strange. He taps a finger against the side of his thigh as he walks.

In that moment, it's as if his eyes darken. I know I need to get out of here before something happens that the both of us might regret.

"I think we should just go to bed and talk about this tomorrow," I tell him, hoping he realizes how scared I am right now.

Instead, he hesitates before swiftly closing the door and clicking the lock shut. The sound has me closing my eyes in defeat. There is *definitely* something wrong with him.

"Bed?"

"Separately," I add, narrowing my eyes.

Silence stretches between us. My heart is beating fast as I try not to think about what my mate is thinking.

Suddenly, Grayson raises his hand up. "I wear this."

It's a ring. Similar to Jasper's, but lighter and newer. It glints under the light menacingly. Just the sight of it has my hands quivering at my side.

"It stops me from going crazy," Grayson tells me. He looks so sincere. It's terrifying.

78

"And with what you're wearing," he mentions, eyes dragging down the entirety of my body, "I don't think I have very much control left."

Before I can let a single word come out of my mouth, he takes long steps toward me, until his face is only centimetres from mine. I can't help but inhale his familiar scent, and get lost in his eyes. He's my mate, but the thought of the wolf that might just be lurking outside right now hovers in my mind.

Slowly, he reaches a hand up, and I let him touch me. It's only a gentle brush of the hand, but the reaction is obvious. He seems to relax, just at the touch of me. He closes his eyes for the briefest second, and when he opens them again, it's as if I'm looking at my mate again. Not the shadow of him.

"You save me," he murmurs, his voice rough and strained. He leans his forehead against mine, looking at me with sparkling eyes.

"Save you?"

Grayson suddenly kneels down, knees touching the floor. I look down at him, as he rests his head against my stomach. I know what he is doing. He's showing me the truth in his words.

"Let me show you," he whispers, his voice almost getting lost within the creases of my shirt. "Let me show you how much I love you."

"No," I breathe. "Not right now."

Slowly, he rises to his feet again and kisses me. At first, I'm stricken with how gentle he allows himself to be. It's enchanting. The magic he wields is knee-weakening.

However, I come to sanity quickly, shoving his chest until he stumbles back from me.

"This is too much too quickly," I tell him.

"You're right. You should get to bed," he says after a moment, looking as if I have thrown a bucket of water over him.

I allow myself to feel comforted as he slings his arms around me to lead me back to my room.

Chapter Seventeen

Grayson

I lean back into the chair, looking out at the sunrise seeping through the tree leaves. Sitting outside on the deck in the mornings is a ritual of mine. Sleeping isn't something I have needed since I became…

Lexia is upstairs, sleeping through the early hours of the morning.

This also happens to be the coolest time of the day, aside from late at night. To me, this is the perfect time to think for a moment. About the uprising, about…

"Someone is up early."

I sit up, scanning the area. The voice is too familiar to forget, but him being here is something I don't prefer to admit, especially with Lexia being so close.

"I'm sure you can relate," I mutter, catching the violet eyes of Jasper.

The moment Lexia mentioned him at the party, our plan finally began. He was supposed to get her back to my Pack, and he succeeded. Although lying to Lexia is something I hate doing. However, I don't want her to worry about me knowing a man who existed centuries ago. It isn't like I want to be in acquaintance with him.

"She nearly caught you last night," Jasper muses, leaning his back against the trunk of a tree. My jaw clenches automatically.

Last night, my plan was to find my brother, Evan, and have him chain me to my bed as he does most nights. The silver stops me from turning, but he was off having a *special* night with his mate.

Eventually, as was I.

I want Lexia to know, but I don't know how she will react when I tell her a part of me is completely uncontrollable. Being a feral and wild creature is something I can't even begin to imagine explaining to her. The things I do when in wolf form are sickening.

Unfortunately, the only man who understands, is Jasper. The Commander of the Phantom Wolves.

It may not be his fault, but calling myself one of them leaves my tongue bitter.

I can tell Jasper is scraping through my mind. "It was Kaden who hired one of my own Phantoms to curse you. Blame him."

Sighing, I run my hand down my face. Looking at Jasper, I know I can't ask him about how to tell Lexia. His mate thinks he died many years ago, and I doubt she thinks it's in the realm of possibility that he would be alive today. If you could call him alive.

"Don't even think about her," Jasper snaps. I raise an eyebrow.

"We have been over this. Stop reading my mind."

"I will when you stop thinking about Thea."

Despite his age on me, he is incredibly protective over his mate. I know of her. Her boyfriend is almost as protective over her as her actual mate. Although, in a fight, I can guess who would win.

Again, Jasper shifts through my mind as if he is reading a book. "At least my mate didn't fuck her assistant."

I stand swiftly. Jasper and I are opposing forces. Ever since he gave me the ring to stop turning into the Phantom Wolf, we have been jabbing at each other constantly. The moment her worthless assistant, Adrian, is mentioned, my anger steps up a level.

"Oh, would you like to talk about Thea and her boyfriend's sex life?" I say, watching the way Jasper stiffens. His hands clench into fists by his side.

I can't wait until our deal is done. His end of the bargain is that he gets Lexia to kill the man behind the uprising. That way, his heart will beat again from his repent, and he can be with his mate. In return, he assists the wolf inside me until I can mark Lexia.

81

"One mark and it will all be over," Jasper says, his voice dangling the alluring possibility closer.

The moment Lexia is marked, the wolf inside me will be trapped forever.

Looking into Jasper's eyes, I can see he is anxious about his heart beating again. The power he wields is something even I'm not fully capable of understanding. His mindreading and time manipulation is one thing, but I'm sure he is hiding other important things from me.

Jasper narrows his eyes at me, but decides not to bring up my thoughts.

Instead, he says, "I will not stop until this deal is complete."

"Do you know anything about Cyprian, or where he may be?" I ask, hating to bring up the name of the man behind the uprising.

Cyprian is young, strong, and manipulative. He is an outsider of the Love Pack, born and raised.

Jasper shrugs. "No, but I have an idea."

Great. Jasper's ideas are always ridiculously extravagant, but they always work. Although usually, his ideas mean he doesn't have to get his hands dirty.

Jasper removes himself from his spot where he is leaning, and begins to pace back and forth before me. "We need allies. He's strong and we won't find him without help from other Alphas," he explains.

"Which Alphas?" I question apprehensively.

Jasper thinks for a moment. "I know you won't like this, but Landon and Malik are important."

I sigh through my nose. Those two nearly ripped each other apart last time they were together. Instead of arguing, I simply nod, letting Jasper continue.

"We need the Alpha of Harmony, Noah…"

My heart drops.

"I don't think Noah and I are on good terms at the moment," I say uneasily, remembering what happened the night of the gala, when I got protective over Lexia. Since then, Noah and my relationship has been on the edge.

82

"You two have to be. Maybe give the Alpha of Desire a call. He might…"

"Don't be stupid! There is no way he would ever accept an offer to help."

Jasper taps his chin as he thinks. "The Alpha of Passion will help."

Isaiah is having issues at his own Pack, but I'm sure the Alpha will be willing to help.

As I begin to feel better about the situation, I catch Jasper's gaze. I know *exactly* whom he is thinking about. We may be on good terms now, but I would rather not have him hanging around Lexia.

"Kaden, Alpha of Vengeance, will be our biggest hope of finding Cyprian!"

I hate having to agree with him. "Fine. What about Lexia?" I ask.

Jasper seems to have forgotten the most important puzzle piece to this game. He hops up the steps, and comes to stand directly in front of me. This suggests that he is only going to propose something I'm not going to agree with.

"I'll take her back to my Pack while you find Cyprian. She will be safe while you are out with business," Jasper says, his voice so suggestive it's convincing.

"Still, I'll have to tell her what I am," I confirm.

Jasper looks doubtful, but nods. I'm not sure if I'm ready to send Lexia to the Devotion Pack.

"Good talk," Jasper says as if he is bored with the conversation. I watch him turn and walk off into the forest. Where he goes, I don't care.

I have to see Lexia.

***

Lexia

I awake to the sudden crash of the bedroom door being swung open by Grayson. A look of determination is etched into his face. As I sit up, I watch him as he approaches the bed. I take a moment to rub the sleep from my eyes and push my hair back.

"We need to talk," Grayson says, as if I couldn't tell already from the expression on his face.

He looks beautiful this morning. His hair is messy from his hand constantly running through it.

"It's a bit early isn't it?"

Grayson takes a seat by my side. "It's important you don't freak out," he tells me.

Instantly, his words have the opposite effect to what he intended. My heart flutters at the insinuation of bad news.

"Lexia, I'm a Phantom Wolf."

Chapter Eighteen

I stare blankly at Grayson as he waits for me to respond to the information he just dumped on me. Phantom Wolf. Phantom Wolf. Phantom…

For some reason, the idea of him being a Phantom Wolf makes perfect sense. The picture of the wolf plastered to his wall. That has to be him. That's the reason why he wandered out into the forest at night.

"You can't read minds, can you?" I ask, remembering the abilities Jasper has. Grayson frowns, taken aback by how calm I'm being about this.

I can't explain my feelings. As I stare into Grayson's eyes, I feel nothing but understanding and I don't know why. The idea of him being almost dead in some strange, almost magical way should have frightened me tremendously. I think he's more worried about this than me.

"No, I can't read minds," he says carefully. "You seem okay with this."

I shrug, almost too casually. "You could say I know another…"

"Jasper," he finishes for me. I gape at him.

He knows Jasper. My mouth hangs wide open, and I stare at him as if he's lying to me. I can't believe I didn't see their alliance coming from a mile away.

"You *did* see him at the party!"

Grayson only nods.

"So, if you're a Phantom Wolf, you're basically dead…" I say, hinting for clarification. Grayson reaches out, placing a hand on my knee.

"No. I have only been cursed for a little amount of time. Unlike Jasper, I have not matured into my possible powers, whereas he has had centuries to perfect the art of magic. Neither of us are truly dead, but we cannot be alive, at the same time."

My eyebrows crease instantly in confusion. "What?"

"Jasper told you about his repent. Well, our forms of recovery are different. I shall allow you to kill the man behind the uprising, who Jasper has been wanting dead for a very long time. Once he is dead, Jasper's heart will beat again. And then, I will mark you, and I will contain the wolf in me forever," Grayson explains.

The wolf. The crazed, hungry-for-vengeance-looking creature on Grayson's wall. Just by the look in his eyes, I can tell the Alpha is pained by mentioning it.

"I understand," I tell him. Maybe I don't fully, but all I know is that I have to agree. I *have* to help. This is where all my training to be a leader comes in, and I want nothing more than to use it against the man behind the uprising. Despite the determination written across my face, Grayson expresses nothing but surprise.

"I still can't believe you're not screaming in fright."

"I trust you," I tell him, admiring the way the Sun through my window illuminates his entire being. I reach out, cupping the side of his face, feeling his smooth cheek beneath my fingertips.

He softly smiles. "There's something else. I need you to leave, to go to the Devotion Pack with Jasper."

I don't expect him to utter those words.

"The man behind the uprising is named Cyprian. He was once a member of the Love Pack, but turned volatile. The only way we are going to find him is…"

He breaks off, but I understand. He wants me gone because he's going to be working with Alphas.

"You'll be safe in Jasper's Pack," Grayson promises. The idea of leaving this Pack is unnerving. I'm starting to see this place more as home.

Grayson's hand clenches my thigh, tightening over my leg through the sheets. I'm naked under these sheets. My body is still unable to handle the heat, and I don't want Grayson to have the image of me naked in his head just yet.

When he slides his hand further up my thigh, as if the fabric between us is no bother, I press it to my body nervously.

"Since when were you shy?" He questions, but his voice is suggestive. His eyes are a-flicker with teasing amusement.

He leans his body over mine, bringing our faces closer. Just looking at him could replenish a tired soul. I want to do more than just see my mate. I hate myself for becoming attached to him already.

"Patience is the key to success," I whisper, slapping the hand that hovers too close to the edge of my sheet. One simple tug on his end could have me completely revealed to his eyes.

He smiles and brushes his lips against my jaw. His touch makes my back slightly arch, and my eyes close. He notices. I can tell by the way the free hand grabs onto my hip. Before I can pull his lips to mine, he jumps away, winking as he stands.

"Get dressed and meet me downstairs."

As I sit up, I want to growl at him while I'm still holding the sheet to my chest. I'm not going to give him the satisfaction of hearing me beg for him, but by the way he looks at me as he wanders out of the room, I am considering it.

***

"I don't know why I didn't freak out more," I voice my feelings to Jasper, as we drive down a narrow straight road.

We are heading to the Devotion Pack. The drive will take us a good 27 hours. We have only been on the road for five minutes and I'm bored. All I have to think about is the sad departure from Grayson.

"Freak out about what?"

"Grayson being like you," I say, not wanting to say the words 'Phantom Wolf.'

Jasper chuckles and I glance at him. The Sun is high in the sky, beating in through the window. Jasper driving a car is an amusing sight. It's just too *normal* for him.

"The Alpha of Freedom and I are nothing alike. Dead, we may be, but I am stronger."

I narrow my eyes at him. I was about to mention something about being humble, but Jasper is quick to respond.

"If I were not strong, would I have been able to entice a spell over you?" He asks with a serious tone. I just stare at him, unable to speak.

He gives me a sideways glance. "It was a simple spell to ensure the transition of Grayson's information about being a Phantom Wolf into your mind went smoothly. It will only last for another few hours. It was to open your mind up a little. Help your body accept the idea."

Everything slots into its rightful place in my mind, and I hardly question it. The spell. Jasper smiles knowingly.

"That is simple magic. I am much more powerful than simple mind manipulation."

I want to ask more questions about his powers, but I hold back. I'm positive he wouldn't tell me anyway, and I don't want to receive any more information until I'm in my right mind.

Therefore, without worrying, I lean my head back, hoping to sleep the time away.

Chapter Nineteen

I don't wake up until the Sun is setting. Jasper is still driving and not saying a word. He seems to be thinking as we cross the land toward his Pack. I've never seen the Devotion Pack before, and I never thought I would have to.

It was a place, I was warned, not ever to go to. Almost abandoned, with only small towns of low populations to speak of, and it was known for the upheaval that happened many years ago. All thanks to Phantom Wolves.

Rubbing my eyes, I sit up. The clock mounted into the dash reads 4:07 PM. I've slept for five hours.

"How far away are we?" I ask. My voice is shaky from sleep.

Despite the time that has passed, he still looks as awake as he was when we started. Eyes bright and skin glowing, he looks exactly like the Alpha that died centuries ago.

"Quite far," he says softly. The Sun reflects off the dark specks that sit at the edges of his irises.

With a huff, I lean back against my seat. Jasper smiles and the edges of his lips tip up as he notices my frustration.

"Check the clock," he murmurs as he swiftly turns a sharp corner on the road. Glancing at the clock, I'm taken aback. 5:12 PM.

"What the…"

Jasper smiles. "Look again."

Now, it reads 6:13 PM. I blink a few times, wondering for a brief second if I'm losing it.

"Your clock is broken."

He chuckles as he nods his head towards the window to get my attention. Following his gaze, I see that the Sun has sunken lower towards the horizon, and the scenery around us has gotten denser. Jasper even has his headlights on as we drive.

"How did you do that?" I ask warily.

He grins. "Magic."

The idea of this being magic frightens me because the moment I blinked, the sky was dark and the clock read an hour later.

"How?" I question.

He sighs, as if gathering the words to explain is a horrendous challenge. "I stop your mind for a moment. I cease it. For what feels like a split second of time for you, is around an hour for me. Your body is wielded by my magic, so for those minutes that tick by, you don't exist."

I stare at him as the words slowly sink in. I can feel Jasper reading the questions in my mind.

"It isn't difficult. The closer we get to my Pack, the stronger my magic becomes. For those moments I take your existence from this earth, I continue driving."

Again, I'm numb. It takes a moment for the feeling to pass, and I can tell it's Jasper's spell making me accept what he is telling me.

"How strong can you get?" I ask, filling the space of silence in the car.

Jasper looks a little uneasy before saying, "Very."

I sit back for a second. Instead of being scared of the man who has casually hinted that he's made me not exist for a couple hours, I'm calm. I wonder if I'll wake up tomorrow in such a state of shock.

"Once the spell wears off, you will not experience any rush of feelings. You will not fear me for who I am, or what Grayson is," Jasper confirms.

His words are somewhat relieving, but I'm not sure how being away from Grayson is going to affect my sanity. I know my emotions will be intact, despite the Alpha of Devotion's meddling.

"So, how will killing this Cyprian guy help you?"

"Grayson and I are both Phantoms. I may be more powerful, but he has direct contact to the Moon Goddess."

My eyes widen. The spell could only do so much to keep the shock from my expression.

"That's only mildly terrifying," I say.

"If he dies, I will be granted the passage of speech to the Goddess. She will grant me my repent," Jasper explains as his fingers grip the steering wheel tightly.

"Can you make time pass again?" I ask him.

When I blink, the Sun is now rising, and we are parked in front of a giant concrete wall.

The Devotion Pack. We made it.

***

Grayson

"How's Mara?"

I carefully watch Isaiah, Alpha of Passion, speak lowly to Kaden, Alpha of Vengeance, from across the table.

"Well, we finally convinced her parents that us being mated was the Moon Goddess' decision," Kaden replies.

"Do you believe that?"

"Not for a second."

I clear my throat, getting everyone at the table's attention. Six Alphas sit before me, and each one of them wants to find Cyprian.

"Thank you all for coming. I know there are rifts in some lines of peace at this table."

I notice Landon, Alpha of Power, and Malik, Alpha of Love, exchange ice-cold glances.

"But we can all admit that we have come together to find Cyprian."

"And then kill him," Kaden adds. The Alpha Vengeance wants anyone who once crossed him dead.

"No, we only find him," I reply.

"How unsatisfactory," the Alpha of Desire mutters. He is looking at his fingers as he leans casually back in his chair. Coming from the Alpha who dabbles with satisfaction, whose words radiate across the table. When he glances up, he catches my gaze with his glinting, golden eyes.

"Trust me. You will all be doing yourselves a favor not getting involved with him!"

"True," Isaiah says. "My Pack is in enough trouble as it is. I will assist you today, but that is as far as I can extend my hand."

This is unfortunate since Isaiah is one of the best Alphas for this job. His Pack is currently undergoing rebellion by its own making, and he has handled it better than any Alpha could.

"I will help you for as long as you need," Landon counters, and I nod gratefully at him.

Malik is on his feet in a second. "Me too. Don't forget about me."

"Thank you, Malik," I say, hoping he will sit down and stop embarrassing himself. All the other Alphas seem to understand the immaturity that Malik holds.

"As for those who have mates at home?" Kaden asks.

Everyone looks a little caught off guard. He is the only one here, aside from me, who has their mate, but he is the only one who has his mate marked.

"It will be fine," Rylan snaps. "You should be able to handle your mate by now."

Still, the Alpha of Vengeance and the Alpha of Purity have not made amends. They stare at each other, hatred mirrored in each of their eyes.

I stand, bracing my hands against the desk. "Shall we begin?"

Chapter Twenty

Lexia

"Welcome to my home," Jasper says as we walk through the front door.

After dumping my duffel bag onto the ground, I look around. Jasper's home is impressive. I am not sure if it is the Devotion Pack fashion or not, but everything is furnished lavishly. As if he is impressing royalty.

"It's pretty old, so watch your step," he calls out as he strides down the hallway. I am sure that if his foot fell through an old board, his magic would be enough to save him.

He had told me that his magic gets stronger within his Pack and I see it, an unexplainable force that swirls around him.

"How old?" I ask as I place one foot nervously in front of the other. If I fall through the floor now, I doubt I will be able to make it up again without Jasper's help. I am not giving him the satisfaction.

"As old as me."

Jasper still hasn't told me exactly how old he is. He always tells me centuries, but I don't know the truth.

He leads me into what I assume to be his lounge room. Dressed in dark tapestries and fabric, the room looks exactly where a brooding Alpha, who casts magic whenever he feels necessary, might be found. I watch Jasper sink into a nearby couch that has a woven, purple blanket draped over it.

"So, what now?" I question as I slowly take a seat on the edge of an armchair. The feeling of the fabric is rich and soft against my skin.

Jasper catches my gaze. "You stay here, where you're safe."

I have no doubt Jasper has an arsenal of tricks he can use against Cyprian, but the mention of him having the ability to talk straight to the Moon Goddess is frightening. Sometimes I have doubts about her existence. But now…

"What if he finds me here?" I ask. The thought sends shivers up my spine.

"He won't," Jasper replies. Something flickers in his eyes and the look on his face makes me want to recoil in fear. "But if he does…"

My heart stops.

"He cannot take one step into my house without burning to death. Years of my own magic has prepared for a moment like this," he explains.

A moment like this? A moment where a girl like me makes a stupid mistake and riles up an entire Pack. I had fuelled his ideas at the right time. I had fallen into a trap I didn't know existed. Now, I am a target.

"So, you're telling me I am stuck here until Grayson finds him?"

Jasper nods. "You may find there are many things about my home that can entertain you."

I've never felt so trapped in my life. The shadows haunting every corner seem to crawl closer, like tendrils wanting to wrap around my neck. Claustrophobia has never been something I have ever dealt with, but right now, it is attacking me from every side.

Jasper notices and alarm surfaces in his eyes as my breathing quickens. He leans forward, placing the palm of his hand on my bare thigh. His hand is ice-cold, but instantly, I can feel the effects of his touch. Magic unfurls from his fingertips, coursing under my skin. The calming effect hits me slowly, and I relax into the couch as the claws around my neck release.

"Your abilities scare me sometimes," I tell him, taking a deep breath in. I wonder what his mate will think of his powers.

He softly smiles and I can tell he read my mind. He definitely felt fear when it came to his mate and his powers.

"I'm not going to trap you in this house," he tells me, bringing the subject back to the situation at hand. "I can take you to visit the nearest town if you would like."

***

The town is small, with only a few shops lining a two-lane road.

"It's basically deserted," I note, as Jasper and I walk side-by-side down the street. We pass by a secondhand clothing shop, and a few other small, run down places.

Jasper nods. "Not many people live here. They don't take too well to strangers, so I suggest we don't stop and talk to any."

We keep walking until we reach a small diner. Jasper grabs my arm with such force that it makes me jump.

"Not there."

"Why not?"

"My mate…"

Thea.

He starts pulling me backwards and a look of stricken disaster paints his face. We made a mistake coming this far down the road.

Suddenly, the door jingles and two girls walk out. Both are wearing matching dusty, pale-blue dresses with frilly white aprons strapped around the front. They are happily engaged in conversation with wide smiles on their faces. Even though they are matching, one sticks out more than the other does though…

Her eyes are a light hazel that blends with her brown hair. The red in her cheeks gives her a look of youthfulness. That must be Thea.

Jasper looks at me, alarmed at the presence of his mate. He grabs my shoulder, looking at me with eyes wider than ever. The calculating, smart Alpha I knew is gone and replaced by a flighty, anxious individual.

"Kiss me."

"Sorry?" I ask shockingly.

"Before she sees," he says hurriedly.

Before I can protest, Jasper pulls me to him and our lips meet.

***

Grayson

"I just don't get it."

Asher, Alpha of Desire, sighs irritably.

"Why is there a Desire Pack?" Alpha Malik questions.

"What do you feel when you fuck all those girls who aren't your mate?" Asher snaps, running a hand back through his dark hair.

We are all sitting in a car. I am driving and Kaden is sitting in the passenger seat. Landon, Asher, and Malik are stuffed into the back. I thought putting Landon away from Malik would solve the issues, but I am obviously mistaken.

"Can you shut it?" Kaden grumbles, looking out the window. I don't feel bad in the slightest for making him sit next to Malik.

We are between the Desire Pack and Devotion Pack. Cyprian is known to draw his power from Jasper's Pack, so we decide this would be the best place to start our search. Once we find his stronghold, it will be Lexia's job to infiltrate.

It's only been three days since I've seen Lexia and I miss her terribly. I want nothing more than to turn around and drive to the Devotion Pack, but she's safer there with Jasper than with me.

The sound of tussling in the back gets my attention.

Kaden's hand is around Malik's neck. Malik only smiles, ice-blue eyes glinting with amusement while Kaden's reflect utter anger.

"Say one more thing about Mara's body," Kaden growls, hands tightening around Malik's neck. I'm surprised the man could even breathe. "I dare you!"

"It's tight…"

I slam the brake on, forcing Kaden to let go of Malik so he can brace himself. Landon, who was sleeping, wakes with a start.

"Stop arguing! We are here to find Cyprian, not kill each other!" I snap, catching all of their eyes in the rear-view mirror.

Kaden's jaw clenches as he reluctantly sits back in his seat.

"Look," Landon says suddenly.

I look where his pointing. A car is flipped on its back in the distance, and I notice a figure sitting right by it. A girl.

As we get closer, she stands. A cut is carved into her forehead and blood is dripping down her face. She looks scared.

I pull over to check on her. Of course, Malik is first to catch a glance at the petite, blonde-haired woman. Before I can stop him, he swings the door open before the car even stops.

"Malik to the rescue," Asher mumbles, as the Alpha rushes instantly to the girl's aid.

Chapter Twenty-One

Lexia

Ever since Jasper had told me he was not interested in me, I had not thought twice about him. Never in a million years would I have thought he would kiss me randomly in the middle of the street.

It wasn't an innocent kiss either. One hand winds into my hair and his fingers press against the base of my skull. His other hand holds the small of my back, forcing me against his body. I am stuck, lips pressed against his.

I know why he is doing this. He is hiding himself from her.

"Get a room," Thea's friend mutters as the two walk past us.

My eyes are open enough to see Jasper looking toward Thea. The moment she glances back over while walking away, I close my eyes. Trying, for Jasper's sake, to look like a typical, young couple.

The moment the two have disappeared around a corner, we push away from each other and I take in a deep breath.

"I'm sorry about that."

The feeling of his lips still sting on mine, like a lingering feeling of regret. *If Grayson finds out…*

"Couldn't you have used magic?" I question. A painful expression graces his face for a moment.

"I freaked out. It rarely happens," he admits. His only weakness is his mate, and I can see why. Being in her presence for not even a minute had him worrying, as if he might get down on his knees and admit that they are mates.

Jasper and I don't talk about the kiss after that.

He brings me back to the house, and says he has something else to do within his Pack. Once again, I am left lounging around a stranger's house with nothing in mind to do. He said his house was entertaining, but after scoping the place out, I find it to be quite the opposite.

Suddenly, I hear someone messing with the front door. Jasper hadn't mentioned anything about a visitor, but this doesn't sound like someone visiting. This sounds like someone is breaking in…

Mustering up some courage, I walk over to the door and open it, ready to beat down any intruder.

Rather than the ax murderer I was expecting to find, a young police officer is standing there. He is dressed from top to bottom in a pristine, black uniform. He is very handsome. Not like Grayson or Jasper handsome, but still attractive enough to captivate someone at first glance. He catches me staring at his badge. His name is Luca.

We share glances for a brief second. His eyes are a brooding hazel and his hair is a light brown, almost blond. He wears it perfectly smoothed back.

"May I help you?"

After he stares down my body, he looks over my shoulder. He is trying to see if there is anyone else in the house.

"Who are you?" He questions. I don't think I will ever get used to the Devotion Pack accent. The pronunciation of words is silky. As if words are always sitting on the edge of their tongues and at the backs of their throats.

"Who are you?" I reply.

His eyes find my body again. "Do you know this is private property?"

"I was given permission to stay here by the owner."

As the words escape my lips, I turn around to see what he is looking at. To my horror, the lavish house I had been staying in has vanished. Instead, a rotting shell of a house now surrounds me.

If things couldn't get any worse, I look down at my body and to my embarrassment; I'm now completely naked in front of this complete stranger.

"I'm arresting you for trespassing."

The rest of Luca's words are drowned out by one thought mulling around in my head.

I'm going to kill Jasper.

***

Grayson

I don't even get a foot out of the car before Malik completely changes persona. The teasing boy is gone, only to be replaced by the Alpha of Love in full personification.

"Someone works quickly," Kaden mutters beside me.

Malik is already helping the girl up, whispering something in her ear to make her laugh. He may be the biggest idiot out of us all, but I don't think anyone could get a girl into bed as quick.

Asher doesn't look fazed by the unfolding situation as he steps nonchalantly out of the car. "As much as I enjoy the smell of a woman turned on, I don't appreciate anyone else committing to a side-of-the-road pick-up near me."

Landon chuckles as he walks towards her car, which is wrecked in the ditch. I inspect the accident from a distance. Blood dribbles down her leg and from the gash on her forehead as she stands. Her arm is locked around Malik's shoulders for support. I notice Malik whisper something in her ear, which she proceeds to blush about. I glare pointedly at the foolish Alpha.

"What? I'm comforting her," he excuses, giving me a subtle wink.

Asher rolls his eyes and wanders off to check the car with Landon. Kaden stoops down, checking the girl's injuries.

"Thank you so much," she gushes as our eyes meet. Tears swim in her pitch-black eyes. They are darker than Kaden's, and that's saying something. "I didn't think anyone would stop."

"What's your name?" Kaden asks as he inspects her knee closely.

She pauses. "Lily."

She said it as if it was a foreign word that she wasn't used to saying. Perhaps it is because two Alphas are currently fondling her; one at the leg, the other at the forehead.

"Don't worry, you're safe now," Malik murmurs, his voice mixed with hints of seduction.

She looks at him gratefully, and I want to sigh. "So, where are you from?"

Lily meets my gaze. For a moment, it feels as if she has taken hold of my soul, and the vulnerable feeling of her being able to crush it with her mind passes through me.

"Where were you going?" I repeat when she doesn't answer, my voice hard as ice.

"The Desire Pack," she says confidently, getting Asher's attention from the car. He doesn't acknowledge it; as if he knows something he isn't telling us.

We end up offering her a ride to the Pack. After disputing Malik's claims that she should sit on his lap, we let her sit in the front seat, and make Malik lie down on the floor in the back. As much as it annoys Malik, it is the most comical thing any of us have witnessed so far on this trip.

"This is stupid," he mutters as he pushes Kaden's foot away from his face. Kaden smiles as he moves his foot from Malik's face to his crotch.

"Watch it! My penis has a lot more to live for. You already found *your* mate."

"Trust me Malik, my mate appreciates mine every morning and every night," Kaden mutters.

"Can we not talk about this with a lady in the car?" Asher says as I meet his gaze in the rear-view mirror. I gratefully nod and he understands that mate talk is hard for me.

My phone rings and it makes us all jump. Without thinking twice, I answer it and the sound of Jasper's voice melts through the line. "I may or may not have gotten your mate put in jail. She is also naked."

101

Chapter Twenty-Two

I drop the phone from my hand as I force the car to the side of the road. I'm not sure what is worse: my mate being in jail, or the idea of her being naked in front of someone else. I can't hold back the growl that is surfacing in my throat.

"What the…"

Kaden cuts me off as I pull immediately onto the gravel on the side of the road. Lily braces her hands against the dash in a wild attempt to stop herself from slamming her head against it.

"Are you crazy? You could have killed us!" Malik snaps as I frantically turn the steering wheel.

"We have to go back to the Devotion Pack."

Before I can get back on the road, Lily steps out of the car in a spectacle of bandages and blonde hair. Despite my impulse to press my foot flat against the accelerator, I step out of the vehicle to go after her.

"I can't go there," she says as she walks down the gravel road. My eyes roll. Perhaps I should just leave her be.

I am about to commit to this decision, but Lily turns around sobbing. It's an hysterical, ear-piercing sound that wrenches my insides.

As always, Malik comes straggling from behind. He always has to be the knight in shining armour. As he approaches her, her knees weaken and he catches her in his arms. He cradles her gently against him.

"You don't understand," Lily mutters through her sobs.

I hear Asher get out of the car from behind us.

"I have to turn around," I tell her and I watch her face fall. "I am sorry."

"I will pay you if you take me back to the Desire Pack," she tells me, tears still brimming in her eyes. She steps forward, dismissing Malik's arms that are around her. Her gaze is relentless, stripping me bare as she strides a few steps toward me, closing the gap between us. I narrow my eyes uneasily.

"We don't need your money," I tell her firmly.

I stay as still as possible, as a smile suddenly appears on her face. The entire group of Alphas don't say a word, as Lily runs the tip of her index finger down my chest.

"It doesn't have to be money I pay you with," she tells me. The suggestiveness in her voice has a kind of sick undertone.

I push her hand off my chest and she stumbles backwards. Instead of falling straight onto the ground, she falls into Asher's arms. Her own Alpha.

"There's only one place we are willing to send you," Asher mutters.

Lily whines and moans in his arms in protest, as if his very touch is the most painful thing to experience. "Let me go!"

"And that place is hell," Asher says simply.

Before any of us can say a word, Asher places his hands on either side of her head and swiftly snaps her neck.

Stunned, I watch as her lifeless body falls straight onto the ground.

The pretty, petite girl of total innocence begins to transform. Grey hair sprouts from her head, the blonde strands dying and curling up. Her youthful appearance diminishes, and her skin ages right before our eyes. Her back arches into a hump, and her limbs start to shrink. Her whole being becomes brittle with age.

Malik turns around and vomits into the ditch behind us.

"Uh…" Kaden drawls as he takes a step out of the car. All of us remain frozen in shock as Asher casually kicks the body into a ditch.

"I had a feeling," he murmurs.

I cannot place what I have just witnessed into words. I just watched the Alpha of Desire kill one of his own Pack members as if it were nothing. Then, in horror, I witnessed this woman drastically age before my eyes.

"Care to explain?" Malik sputters. I notice him averting his gaze from the body.

"That woman is what you call a succubus."

"A what?" Malik questions with an oblivious look across his face.

"A female demon that seduces men to take their soul. A man's soul restores their youth and beauty. She was planning to kill us all…"

"How did you know?" I ask.

"Succubi are creatures who lurk in the shadows in my Pack. They haunt the dreams of many Pack members. Recently, many men in my Pack have gone missing. We assume they are the culprits."

Asher kicks the lifeless body again. My respect for Alpha Asher is quite high. He's a lot older than I am, and handles his Pack as best he can.

"So, she uses magic to appeal to men's darkest desires?" Kaden asks, still staring at the woman as if she might come alive and bite at his ankles.

"Due to our proximity to the Devotion Pack, yes," he informs us. "They collect and manipulate men's power."

"Can we continue this conversation in the car? We have to go and get Lexia, now!"

***

Lexia

I am banging the back of my head against the wall as I anxiously wait in my cell.

"I had to protect the place," Jasper says in a whisper. He had suddenly appeared in my cell in a soundless exposition of atoms and darkness. I had smacked my head against the concrete wall in fright.

104

"I don't want to hear it!"

"I was protecting my home! No one can know the estate still exists!"

"Blah blah…"

"I placed a spell on it long ago to make it seem as if it wasn't truly there. Not in its best form at least."

The bed I'm forced to spend the night on tonight is as hard as rock. I can already tell the amount of sleep I will get is going to be minimal. Nonetheless, they gave me a pillow, which was debated upon at first.

"Did you have to make me naked?" I question.

After arriving in the jail, I was given a sort of delinquent uniform. It is grey and sticks to my body with static electricity.

Jasper sighs. "You had to look like a trespasser. It was the only way to not raise suspicion."

I stop listening after that.

Jasper refuses to get me out because he doesn't want to be seen. He informs me that he has called Grayson.

Goddess protect me from the inevitable wrath that will be my mate.

"That way he can get you out and everything will be fine."

Blinking, I rub my eyes and lay back on my bed. It could have been made of nails, and been just as uncomfortable as this.

Perhaps Jasper got the message as he vanishes without a trace. I'm grateful that he is finally gone because my anger and embarrassment cannot be subdued by his excuses.

How long will I have to wait for Grayson?

***

I must have been asleep for hours. As I open my eyes, the room is dark and only a small trace of moonlight seeps through the barred window. I roll over to assess my surroundings, and I am surprised at who I see standing in front of the iron cage. Adrian.

The last time we had seen each other was at the party. It feels like ages ago. The expression on his face looks anxious.

"Lexia," he says in a whisper.

"What are you doing here?"

"I heard what happened and I came immediately," he explained. "They took your clothes?"

A strange thing to bring up at this time, but I don't question his reasoning. I see his gaze drift to my neck.

"Did they take your necklace?"

My hand finds it instantly: the last remaining part of me that belongs to the Discipline Pack. My parents gave it to me for my 11th birthday. Luckily, I've kept it round my neck ever since.

"Don't let them take it," he demands, his voice deepening.

"How did you get in here?" I question. "Why come now, when…"

Adrian shakes his head. "Give me your necklace, before they take it."

I snap the necklace from my neck without hesitation. Without even thinking twice. I want to keep it safe.

"So, are you here to get me out…" my sentence cuts off as Adrian's hand clasps around my necklace.

His eyes go cold and distant as he looks over my shoulder at the wall behind me. Before my eyes, I watch a halo of dark blue smoke rise from the floor at his feet.

I gasp, stumbling back a few steps as it envelops him. In a split second, Adrian is gone and an unfamiliar man takes his place. His lips tilt in a winning smile. "Lexia, I'm glad to finally meet you. I've been looking for you for a very long time…"

Chapter Twenty-Three

"Who the hell are you?"

I have just watched my assistant transform into I man I have never met. A man who looks strikingly similar to...

Malik?

His eyes are the same crystal blue with the same glazed-over expression that draws you in. A gaze that seduces you into thinking that it is only meant for you. A specific trait that only belongs to one Pack. The Love Pack.

His hair is longer than I have seen on a male for some time, shoulder-length and thick. He wears it neatly slicked back, just like Malik, but his face is completely different. Less youthful, and more angular.

I keep trying to convince myself that it is Malik, but I know who he is. I just don't want to admit it.

His lips smile in triumph. "I am sure your darling mate informed you of who I am."

My necklace dangles between his fingers, and the sunlight from the small window reflects off the gold tint.

"Cyprian," I whisper, his name distasteful on my tongue. "How did you find me?"

"I found you the moment you stepped away from Kaden's Pack. The right moment to approach you didn't present itself until now."

I hate his voice. It is so proud and confident. That gentle, melodic sound that caresses your insides in a way that makes your skin crawl.

Cyprian paces around the cell with calculated steps. His pacing makes me uneasy.

"Stalker," I snap. I want to be angry, but I am terrified.

He chuckles. "I wasn't stalking, my dear. I was waiting for an opportune time."

My heart stops as he stares at me, stripping down my confidence layer by layer.

"I think you should go. I am not interested in anything you have to say," I say while trying to keep my voice as calm as possible.

"I am sure you will be pleased with what I have to offer…"

"Doubt it," I cut in sardonically, narrowing my eyes at him.

A cloud of smoke appears at his feet again, swirling around his limbs as it rises, until it swallows him whole.

"You don't have much choice." As the words echo against the cell walls, I cannot see where he is. I cower against my bed in fear.

"You can't make me do anything," I growl into the darkness.

All of a sudden, I hear a low chuckle before he appears before the edge of my bed.

How did he do that?

"Is that right? Do you not realize you just gave me a piece of you," he tells me, dangling the necklace in front of me. "And you have no idea what I can do with it."

Something inside me snaps. I reach forward. My hand swipes for the delicate chain I worship, but my fingers only just graze it. Cyprian grasps my hand within his own, thrusting me toward his body.

I gasp as my chest presses against his. Cyprian looks down at me with eyes alight with victory.

"I am in control now," he murmurs.

I want to do *something*, but I am paralyzed.

"Get off me," I snap, finding my voice. I push my elbow against him and kick my foot up, but he catches it in mid swing. The feeling of being trapped only adds fuel to the fire.

I must escape.

"You're stronger than this, Lexia," Cyprian says in my ear. "Give me a reason not to take you away from your mate forever."

This time, I know what I have to do. I twist my foot around his lower leg, pushing him off balance enough to elbow him in the stomach, hard. He lets me go, and a part of me can't help but think he did it on purpose.

"Good," he mutters as I fall back onto my bed.

"Get out!"

"I could have overpowered you," Cyprian says in amusement. "But I can tell this has a lot more meaning to you," he muses, holding up the only possession of mine that matters to me.

I go to scoff at his words, but a loud bang from outside my cell makes me jump. Cyprian, on the other hand, isn't fazed by it.

"Where the hell is Lexia? She's my mate!"

"Grayson!" I shout as I almost collapse from instant relief.

"We will meet again soon, Lexia. I promise." With his final words, Cyprian vanishes without a trace. A cloud of thick, blue smoke follows in his wake.

The door to my cell opens with such angst and impatience that the sound of the metal door hitting the concrete wall makes my ears ring. Grayson strides into the room. I know if I were standing, my knees would have weakened to the point of collapsing.

We lock gazes. Silver on green.

"I can't believe it," I hear Grayson say, his voice breathy as he drinks in the sight of me in a prison cell. Me wearing a prison outfit like some sort of delinquent.

Grayson rushes over to my bedside, and lifts me into his arms. My body goes limp from his touch. Without hesitation, I place my hands on the sides of his face, and bring his lips to mine. Our kiss is passionate and feverish.

"I'm going to kill Jasper, you know," Grayson says breathlessly, once we finally part ways for air. He still holds me close, forehead against mine so we can relish the sparks between us.

My smile fades. "I just met Cyprian."

Grayson's expression is instantly cold and he begins to ask me questions. "Where is he? How did he find you? Did he hurt you?"

I don't want to tell him about the extent of Cyprian's and my conversation. I know he has a plan, but I don't know how he plans to execute it. I place my hand on my chest, feeling the empty space where my necklace should be.

"No, I'm fine. You just have to promise me you'll find him soon," I say.

Grayson nods. "And when we do, he's dead."

Chapter Twenty-Four

Grayson and I are standing in the lobby of the police station. I listen to him as he explains to the patrol officer why I was on private property. I can tell Grayson is holding himself back from knocking out Luca, the officer who saw me naked.

"Go take a seat and I will go through your paperwork," Luca says gruffly to Grayson.

Jasper strolls casually in behind us, not saying a word. Apparently, he is invisible to anyone other than us. At first, I don't believe it is true. However, my disbelief vanishes as I witness Luca look straight through the Alpha of his own Pack.

It seems to take several hours for Luca to 'look over' my paperwork. I sit with my legs draped over Grayson's, and my head lies heavy on his shoulder. I am beginning to drift off when I hear someone walk through the door.

My mouth nearly falls open at the sight of her.

Thea.

She is carrying a brown paper bag in her hand, and is still wearing her diner uniform. The moment she steps into the room, I notice Jasper tense on the chair beside me as he watches his mate walk right past him. She is heading to the man sitting at the guard station.

"Hey babe, I brought you lunch," Thea says warmly to Luca.

He steps down from his desk, and walks over to her. He grabs her waist to pull her closer. She giggles in delight, dropping the bag onto the desk. She isn't even my mate, but it is still painful to watch her kiss Luca. I glance over at Jasper and I see his eyes are directed at the ground, his expression grim.

"I have work to do, but I will see you later, okay?"

Thea nods before casting a glance at me. I wonder for a moment if she recognizes me from the kiss Jasper and I shared. If she does, she doesn't show it, as she turns and walks straight out the door without a second glance.

***

The moment I walk into Jasper's home, I have the wind knocked out of me as I am greeted by four Alphas.

The Alpha of Vengeance stands by the window, gazing out at the horizon. His arms are crossed over his chest. The Alpha of Love is casually sitting on the couch, and the Alpha of Power is asleep on the armchair.

Last, but not least, the Alpha of Desire is leaning against a bookshelf while reading a thick novel.

"Hope you weren't too bored while we were gone, boys," Jasper proclaims as we walk in, loudly clapping his hands together.

I catch Asher's gaze, letting myself marvel only for a second in the golden light of his eyes. He looks wary of me.

Grayson has his hand protectively on the small of my back, staking his claim. This is his way of silently assuring everyone in the room, but Asher's eyes still linger on me. His gaze is making me nervous and uncomfortable.

"I can tell you kissed him," Asher says suddenly, stilling my blood.

"Me?" Grayson asks in surprise. Asher smiles knowingly, and I wonder if running out of the room is an option right now.

Asher slides his book back on the shelf. "A perk of being the Alpha of Desire is the ability to sense a certain aura. I can see you kissed Alpha Jasper from a mile away, Lexia."

The blood drains from my face, as my mind scrambles trying to find the right answer. Although, it doesn't seem as though Grayson is about to hear it, as he slowly turns to Jasper, eyes colder than ice.

Jasper raises his hands up. "I can explain."

112

He doesn't have the time to say anything before Grayson throws a punch directly at his face. I have no doubt Jasper could have used some sort of magic against the Alpha of Freedom, but to my surprise, he decides to let Grayson hit him across the face.

"I deserve that," he mutters, instantly cupping his face.

"Son of a…"

I step in, wedging myself between a brooding Grayson and a hurting Jasper. "Listen Gray…"

My mate casts his gaze down at me and the look in his eyes sends a chill straight through me. He is furious. It's as if he wants to keeps punching Jasper, but is holding himself back.

"He had to do it. If he didn't, Thea would have seen him and everything would have been ruined for them," I tell him insistently.

Despite my honesty, it makes no difference to Grayson. He is fuming and red in the face with anger. It doesn't help that four other Alphas are staring at us.

"We should go upstairs," I whisper to Grayson as I try to grab his hand. He pulls away from me, and I follow him as he walks down the corridor.

We step into one of the empty bedrooms, which is decorated with large furniture, including a decent-sized bed pressed up against the wall.

I take a seat on the edge of the bed while Grayson paces in front of me.

"I don't get it," he mutters. "Is it because I haven't marked you?"

I make a disconcerting face, brandishing his idea as ridiculous. "It was to protect him. He was caught off guard, and who knows what chaos would have ensued had Thea met the eyes of the man who was supposed to be dead four centuries ago!"

"You don't understand how mad it makes me to know *he* kissed you!"

I reach forward, stopping Grayson in his tracks by grabbing his face between my hands. This forces him to look at me.

"Look, we will find Cyprian, get Jasper's revenge, whatever it may be, and he can go be with his mate," I tell him, my thumbs caressing his cheeks. "Then, we will have all the time in the world together."

Grayson nods, taking a deep breath before whispering, "What would we be doing with all this time?" The teasing hint to his voice is juvenile and playful.

I smile, catching onto the game he is insinuating. "I have an idea. It involves your lips on mine."

Grayson presses his lips softly against mine. Even though his gesture is gentle, it still takes my breath away, rendering me completely open to his unspoken demands.

Suddenly, what began as an innocent kiss starts to become heated. I feel myself falling backwards, only to be caught in the soft clutches of the bed. Grayson looms over me, looking down at me with a gaze as hard as stone.

"I want you," Grayson purrs breathlessly. "I want my mark on your neck, but not here. Not in Jasper's Pack."

I nod frantically. I want to know what the other option is that he isn't saying. His eyes slowly move down my body, as if he is conjuring up what desirable inflictions he wants to place upon me.

It only takes him seconds to undress me. He pauses for a second, as if drinking in my exposed skin.

At that moment, everything I have felt toward mates and Alphas changes completely. Grayson would never leave me, and he would never let another man hurt me. Not like my sister's mate did. I trust him. With not just my life, but also my soul.

Grayson braces himself over me, arms beside my head. "Now I know why your assistant looks at you the way he does."

I roll my eyes.

"Are you really bringing *him* up right now?" I question blandly.

"You will forget about him the moment you start moaning my name," Grayson says, the smile on his face infectious.

My hands curl in his hair, letting the soft strands of midnight black slip through my fingers. His hands are brave, finding my hips, waist, and breasts. The insistence of his kisses and his hands only increases, the breathy whimpers coming from my mouth incentive enough.

I know where he is planning to end this, with the way his index finger traces a faint line down the middle of my stomach toward my core. It is confirmation when he nudges my legs wider with his knee, and his lips fall lower.

I had been with others before and I had felt pleasure with them, but *nothing* like this.

No one could ever compare to the feeling Grayson is giving me. The sparks, the hands, and the lips. Everything about the way he presses his tongue against my sensitive middle has my eyes crossing and my toes curling.

"Grayson," I breathe, digging my fingernails into the bedsheets as his tongue moves in against me.

My muscles tense, as the feeling of release begins to build in my stomach, teasing me, as only Grayson can draw it closer. My mate's name stumbles past my lips, his fingers clenching on my thighs, my back arching as I reach the most mind-blowing climax of my life. All at the hands of one man.

The euphoric feeling comes down slowly as I take deep breaths to calm myself. Grayson looks up at me from between my legs, his expression light and pleased.

As he crawls back up again, coming face-to-face with me, I realize I love him more than I could ever describe.

Chapter Twenty-Five

I can't tell what time it is, and I don't know how long I've been asleep. The open window reveals a faint moonlight, and the air that fills the room is crisp. Grayson is beside me fast asleep. His mouth is parted slightly and his breath is soft.

His arm is slung up the bedpost, bound by a chain made of pure silver. Jasper let him borrow it to control his wolf for the night.

I swallow hard, wanting to reach out and touch the smooth skin of my mate. To feel the sparks under my skin, pulsating through my veins. However, something seems to jerk my hand away from him.

Suddenly, my limbs act as if they don't belong to me. Instead, an unknown force crawls and manipulates my entire being. I try to scream for help, but it is as if someone as sewn my lips shut. My body lunges out of bed without assistance, and I am forced to put my clothes on.

After I'm dressed, I pad down the stairs. Whoever is controlling me is making sure that no one can hear me.

My feet tread softly down the corridor, and I see Jasper in the lounge. He is sitting in an armchair, reading. He doesn't even acknowledge my existence. At first, I think it's blatant ignorance, but as I tiptoe past the lounge, I know he cannot see me.

I try to yell at him for help, but my efforts are useless. Even my throat has ceased to reverberate sound. He remains entranced by his novel as I walk past.

I finally reach the front door, and I make my way outside. My feet are bare as I walk along the dirt road. My heart beats rapidly as I walk through the woods. I begin to panic.

Am I being lead to my death?

Whatever magic has a hold of me could send me straight off the edge of a cliff, and I wouldn't be able to do anything to stop it.

I begin shaking as I walk farther into the woods. My feet are aching from the rough path, and the night is shrouded with a blanket of cold, chilling me straight to the bone.

After what feels like an eternity, I exit the woods and before me lies a paved road. I see a car parked a few feet away, with the back door wide open. My body moves towards the car, and once again, I try to fight. My efforts prove to be useless...

When I reach the car, there is someone sitting in the driver's seat. He doesn't bother turning around in his seat as I slide in. He is wearing black leather gloves, and his fingers are curled around the wheel as I close the door.

***

The driver doesn't talk to me the entire drive, never once taking his eyes off the road. I try to get a glimpse of his face in the rear-view mirror, but the darkness prevents me from seeing his features. All I can see is his thick, brown hair.

We pull up in front of an unfamiliar building that stands tall and narrow over an empty field. The building has no windows, just a blank, wooden wall that stretches up at least three stories.

The driver gets out, closing the door behind him. When he comes to open my door, his facial expression is of surprise. I don't know if it is because of him recognizing me, or because of my reaction when I see him.

It is Cal the Huntsman. The look in his light-brown eyes is of guilt and sorrow. He clenches his jaw as he lets go of my hand, and places his own on the small of my back.

"I know this looks bad," he whispers. "I promise this is not my doing."

"I thought you said we would never have to meet again," I say sourly, finally having the ability to speak again. We walk closer to the house, Cal's hand heavy on my back.

Cal sighs. "Just don't say anything stupid."

I don't have time to ask him what he means as we walk through the front door of the building. The inside is equally as deranged as the outside, empty and desolate.

The moment we arrive into the main room, my head is forced to meet the gaze of Cyprian.

"Welcome to my home, Lexia."

My necklace sits neatly in front of him on a table. His hands are folded over each other, as he looks at me critically.

"You son of a bitch!"

"Such vulgar words from such a beautiful woman," Cyprian says softly, tilting his head as he smiles cruelly.

"Why don't you take a seat?" he says in a pleasant manner, as I am forced to sit down in the seat across from him.

"Thank you for being such a willing participant," Cyprian remarks with a sly hint of amusement in his voice. "And thank you, Cal, for bringing her."

Turning slightly in my seat, I see Cal guarding the door. Despite my confused feelings toward the man that once saved me, I can't help but notice he does looks terrified.

"Don't act as if I want to be here," Cal growls.

He must be under Cyprian's spell as much as I am. How did the skilled Huntsman manage to get himself in this situation?

"I hope you had a good night with your mate," Cyprian purrs. "It sure seemed like it."

"You're sick," I respond with disgust.

"Would you like to know why I brought you here?"

Whatever he wants from me, I will find a way to do the opposite. I will get my necklace back from him, and counter whatever magic he is using to control Cal and me. Then, I will return to Grayson, find Jasper to kill Cyprian, and be done with this mess.

"I am not doing anything for you. I am not a part of this rebellion anymore!"

He chuckles in a way that can only be described as sadistic. "Are you sure about that?"

He stands and strolls over to Cal with his hands tucked behind his back. The Huntsman looks disgusted at Cyprian, but remains still as Cyprian runs a finger down his chin, taunting him.

"If you don't agree to what I propose, I will kill Cal," he asserts. "Then Thea, so I can watch Jasper die a painful death."

My heart stops for a moment, but I keep my expression impassive. Cal's gaze darts to mine, but I can't tell what he is thinking.

Cyprian turns around, walking back to me. He places his hands on my shoulders. "Then, when there is no Alpha of Devotion to protect you, I will kill Grayson."

"What do you want?" I ask without hesitation.

He laughs as he rounds the table again, taking a seat back in his chair.

"One thing," he tells me.

"And what might that be?" I ask, despite being terrified of the answer.

He smiles slightly.

"Mara."

Chapter Twenty-Six

Instantly, I am taken aback by his proclamation.

"Mara? No, I can't. Even if I wanted to, I could never get past Kaden," I say, remembering the way he protects her with his life. The way he will most likely kill anyone if they touch her.

"Do you think I am stupid?" Cyprian ridicules. "I have a plan."

A plan that could potentially go wrong and leave me in the hands of the Alpha of Vengeance.

"Tell me what you want with her first," I barter. Cyprian narrows his eyes at me, as if he is suspicious of what I might do with that information.

"I need leverage over Kaden. I need something that will make him weak, and I have failed to find anything. Until now. That Purity Pack member came into his life and changed everything. Now, I'm going to change the rules to our little game," Cyprian tells me with confidence.

"Kaden is smart. You don't think he will retaliate if you take his mate from him?"

"He won't have time to gather his army before I am securing my allies within his Pack," he says.

"And how to you expect me to get Mara?"

Cyprian chuckles, as if it's an ingenious plan. "She still visits her family in the Purity Pack. Kaden doesn't usually come with her, which is where you come in."

"You want me to intercept her in her own Pack? She's too smart for that."

"She is also innocent. You only have to retrieve her, not convince her. Once she is in my possession, you are free to go."

I don't believe him. My gaze narrows on my necklace on the table.

"Do I get that back?"

He follows my gaze and then a cruel smile taints his expression. "I think this will remain in my possession for safe keeping."

"Deal off then."

How I have the confidence to stand up from my chair and stalk toward the exit, I don't know. As stupid as it is, at least I'm showing him I'm not about to make deals that don't benefit me. Even if he does stop me before I can step one foot out of the room.

"Remember where you came from. I will kill everyone in the Discipline Pack if you so much as step a foot out of line, Lexia. Would you like me to demonstrate with Cal?" Cyprian questions.

Cal's eyes widen with fright as Cyprian approaches him.

"No, I'll do it, on one condition." I cut in.

Cyprian turns to face me again. "And what might that be?"

The thought of bartering with this deranged Love Pack member makes me sick, but I have no choice.

"You leave me alone. You don't correlate me to the rebellion in any way," I say carefully.

I have a plan, a foolish plan that might get me killed, but a plan nonetheless. If Kaden believes me, then I can take down Cyprian and end this.

"Fine."

***

Dawn is starting to set as Cal drives me back to the Devotion Pack.

"You should just drive us far away," I muse, staring out the window.

Cal sighs. "I sacrificed myself for someone," Cal tells me, his voice quiet and reserved. "My Alpha. He wants her and I sacrificed myself to do his bidding."

121

Her? A female Alpha?

Cal catches my gaze in the rear-view mirror, seeing the confusion written all over my face.

"Do you know the story of the Moon Goddess? Cyprian's only ally," Cal asks.

"I do not pray to her, nor does anyone praise her in the Vengeance Pack."

"Millions of years ago, there was a girl. She belonged to a poor family, who loved her very much. Everyone in their small village loved her too, saying she was the personification of all that is pure and beautiful," Cal tells me.

I sit up in my seat, curious.

"Then, one day, something terrible happened. The girl, now a blossoming teenager, fell through time and space. No one knew how this happened, but the village was devastated. The villagers were convinced that the Moon had stolen the beauty from their village."

"How is that possible?" I question.

Cal holds a finger to his lips for a moment. "The girl was stuck in this unknown void, floating and watching. She gazed over her family, unable to age as she watched her village grow. Every night, they would pray for the Moon to return her. This continued through generations, until a stranger came to the village. The villagers told this stranger about a beautiful goddess that belonged to a moon, who everyone prayed to."

"He returned to his city, with word of the Moon Goddess on his lips. The rumour spread and people began to believe in the Moon Goddess. People prayed to her for cures, for happiness, and safety. To their misfortune, their prayers went unanswered, for she did not have the ability to grant such things. Saddened by this, the Moon Goddess wallowed in guilt."

My heart sinks. The poor girl, having to watch her family die, and to hear these people beg for her help.

"When the Great War began, before the Pack Quarter was created, the Moon Goddess still had the greatest soul known to anyone. She sacrificed her soul to bring peace, using herself to create an alliance."

As I look out the window, I notice we are now entering the Devotion Pack.

"This left the Goddess without a soul. Her purity began to fade more and more each day, despite the praise from the Purity Pack."

Cal smiles slightly. "That is where my Pack, the Independence Pack, comes in."

I have heard little about the Independence Pack. I know that it is a Pack deep within the mountains to the south. Apparently, it is so hard to get there that few leave and few come in. This is probably why I have never heard about the female Alpha.

"My prior Alpha would sing to the Goddess, just like her ancestors did. Their beautiful voices brought back the Goddess' purity, and taught her how to heal and bring happiness."

All of a sudden, Cal's expression is full of sorrow. "Cyprian is holding my Alpha's mother, captive. He is using her heart to talk to the Goddess and to manipulate her. He can do so much damage with the Goddess on his side," Cal tells me. "But the Alpha's mother is slowly dying. When she passes, Cyprian will take the Alpha of Independence and use her to continue his malicious plan."

I can tell Cal feels something for the Alpha of Independence. Whether she knows it or not, Cal is doing everything in his power to protect her.

"Then we need to take away that connection," I say.

"You have to get Mara from him. You need to earn his trust."

The Sun has begun to rise as we reach Jasper's house. I tell Cal goodbye, but I have a feeling he knows we will see each other soon.

Chapter Twenty-Seven

Grayson

I don't want to be here.

Right now, I am an innocent creature of prey wandering into a lion's den. As much as I hate this man, I have no other choice.

My gait doesn't falter as I wander straight through his front door. Determination is written all over my features. I keep trying to remind myself that I cannot let him entice me with his lies and manipulation.

I step into a giant room. The back wall is stacked with books up to the roof, and a massive, sparkling chandelier glitters from the ceiling. The chandelier's elegance contrasts to the bleakness of the rest of the room.

In the middle of the room sits a large throne. The man occupying it grins at me with feline amusement.

"Grayson! To what do I owe such a monumental visit?" he questions with valor, jumping to his feet.

His eyes, like a palette of ink, make me feel as if I am staring into a soulless pit of darkness.

"Don't act as if I want to be here," I snap. The man has never done anything against me, but his power is truly frightening.

"You exert such kindness." He skips forward on light steps.

He is wearing a dressed leather jacket, and his cobalt hair is slicked back. He is a man who has never let his old age define him.

"Fate," I growl. "We need to talk."

He raises an eyebrow, clapping his hands together in what could be considered a merry gesture. However, I know that this is not his intention.

"Oh really? I thought the Alpha of Freedom had come over for a cup of tea and a biscuit," he says sarcastically.

I catch his gaze. "I am sure you already know why I am here."

"The Goddess herself can play with dice, but I myself dabble only in chess," he says cryptically, propping his legs up on the armrest on his massive seat.

He smiles cruelly. "You will not find out until the end that I was playing with two Queens."

"Can you talk some sense?" I snap.

He laughs shrilly, swinging his legs back up to press against the back of his chair, so his body hangs upside down. He waves at me from this position, and I have the impulse to shake some sense into him.

"What fun would it be to look into the future, decide our fate now, when I can just listen?"

Fate summons me with a gesture of his fingers. I stride forward, still wary of him.

Fate predicts and chooses the way of life, leaving no room for escape. This man is potentially more dangerous than the Moon Goddess, but he is missing one thing…

"I know what you want," I tell him. He swings back up, sitting normally in his chair. His eyes gleam speculatively.

"And what could you offer the one who has all?" he asks, crossing one leg over the other.

I push my shoulders back, trying to exude some confidence. "Something that will grant you the power that you want, but I need something in return."

The man is a puzzle and everyone who believes in him is aware of this trait. If he is bored, he will play with you, dangle you around like a toy. The trick is to interest him, to put him on a leash before he can put you on his. If you fall to his words, he can torture your mind in unspeakable ways.

125

"Tell me your plans, Grayson," Fate orders, a flicker of doubt still evident in his expression.

"You know of Cyprian," I say.

He nods, sighing deeply. "I am aware."

"I need your help in killing him," I proclaim. His attention is zoned on me, my statement obviously taking him by surprise.

"Are you mad?" he questions. His laugh fills the large space, answering my words with ridicule. "His fate has been written, but I am not the reason for his demise."

I grab Fate's shoulders, enjoying the look of surprise on his face. He isn't used to being touched.

"Why can't you tell me his fate?" I ask, my voice reverberating off the walls.

Fate's expression darkens. "Because of the Moon Goddess, because she can see all. She is the one who receives the praise, not I."

I knew what he meant, mostly. Belief is power and very few believe in Fate. If he were to take the Moon Goddess' spot in the unknown, he would be all-powerful.

"The Moon creates the power the Goddess possesses," Fate says irritably, stepping back a step, so my hands fall from his shoulders. "The Moon stole her in the first place, so tell me how I, someone who is not appreciated, can take her place?"

For me, it isn't about wanting Fate to be in the Moon Goddess' position. It is about Cyprian, and the threat he is to my mate. Fate is the only person I can think that can help me.

"The Goddess wants nothing more than to walk on Earth again and age like normal. The Alpha of Independence told me herself," I say, watching Fate pace in front of me.

"Yes, Faye. Such a beautiful woman," Fate professes.

I sigh deeply. "If we kill Cyprian, then we can set the Goddess free with Alpha Jasper's power and yours combined. We both get what we want."

Fate taps his chin thoughtfully. He knows this is a hard opportunity to pass up.

"You can't fight fate, Alpha, and the Moon selected the girl to rule," Fate says bitterly, turning around to stroll back to his throne.

"Please, you have to help me. Think of everyone you will be saving…"

Fate raises his hand, his back still facing me. My words cease.

"Do you not know that any small twist in the lines of fate will create a completely different outcome? If I were to kill Cyprian, when my fate is not to do so, it could change everything!"

I watch him take a seat back on his throne.

"What if your fate is to do this? Obviously, it is mine to come to you with this proposal. Please, think about it," I tell him.

My hope is that he will think primarily about himself, because if he does, it will aid me in the best way possible.

Chapter Twenty-Eight

Thea

I sit on a bench along the sidewalk a couple houses down from Mara's house.

The Purity Pack is exactly how I imagined it would be. Places of worship are everywhere, and are in better shape than the majority of the houses. The climate is temperate, which is a complete change from the heat in the Freedom Pack and the chill from the Devotion Pack.

Mara lives somewhere along this street. I am still not sure how I am going to get her back to Cyprian, but as long as Kaden doesn't find out, I should be fine.

I was told her address, but I feel as though showing up at her parents' house is going to raise some suspicion. Being smart about how I will approach her is essential.

Mara's house is average and modest. Mara, as the current Luna of the Vengeance Pack, primarily lives within that Pack, instead of the one she was born in, where she used to pray to the Moon Goddess.

Everyone is starting to close his or her curtains as evening begins to set in. Grayson told me they do this, since their religion suggests modesty and self-protection. With everyone isolating themselves for the evening, I am surprised when someone sits next to me. I can't see their face, but I hear an insistent mumbling about the uselessness of this Pack.

I keep my eyes on Mara's house, still thinking about how I am going to get in there.

"These people are going to realize one day that their own Alpha is playing with them, telling them some Goddess lives in the sky when really they are completely delirious..."

Still, I ignore the rambling girl, watching as a black SUV suddenly pulls up outside Mara's house.

"But really, he is just a useless Alpha who doesn't even know how to protect his own Pack..."

I frown, sitting up more on the seat, trying to see who is in that car. The girl on the other side of the bench is trashing Alpha Rylan. Her rambling is starting to get annoying as I try to concentrate on the man stepping out of the SUV.

It's Kaden.

The moment his feet touch the ground, my heart plummets. I was told he wasn't going to be here. Now, my entire plan is in danger of being exposed.

"I'm not even from this Pack," the girl continues, her presence suddenly giving me an idea as Kaden looks around, forcing me to duck my head down in case he sees me.

"I need this," I say quickly as I try to grab the newspaper she is holding. I want it to conceal my face.

The girl looks at me with pitch-black eyes that match her hair, and I know instantly she is from the Desire Pack. Well, originally that is. Instead of willingly handing over the newspaper, she grapples it harder, pulling it back.

"This is mine!"

I don't let go, fingers piercing the fragile paper. "Look, it's the Alpha of Vengeance," I proclaim to her. The diversion works. Not only do I get a handle on the paper, but I also watch as she turns to look at Kaden. Her face pales as she struggles to her feet, and I laugh as I watch her taking off at a swift run down the sidewalk.

I peek over the newspaper, watching Kaden tell a companion of his, who I assume is a guard, to get back into the car. Once the other man listens, Kaden proceeds to walk to the front door of Mara's house. He is immediately let inside.

I set the newspaper down, but not before looking at it first. The news story that girl was looking at takes me by surprise.

Alpha Rylan is under public scrutiny after allegations of his disbelief of the Moon Goddess

Is that their biggest news? I can't imagine Rylan doing anything to harm his Pack. I suppose some people will find anything to print.

I am about to stand and admit defeat for my mission when the sound of a door slamming brings my gaze back to the house.

Mara is slinging a coat over her shoulders as she runs across the road. I stand, watching as she holds her head in her hands, and I become aware that she is crying.

This is my chance.

"Mara!" I call out. Only the endgame is in sight.

She pauses as her glacier eyes lined with tears find my gaze. "Lexia?"

I remember when we first met; we have quite the past. My reign within the Vengeance Pack was at its peak, and she decided to confront me. She knew at the time that Grayson was my mate, and was convincing me to give up on the Pack and be with him. After I saved her ass from a crazy man, we have been on good terms.

I am about to ruin that.

"Are you okay?" I ask, crossing the road to her.

"Yes, I'm fine. What are you doing here?"

"Well, Grayson and I are visiting. He is doing some work with Alpha Rylan."

She nods thoughtfully, not looking as if she wants to question it. Frankly, something else is on her mind, which is going to help me get her back to Cyprian.

"You look sad," I note, hoping to coax whatever has made her cry out of her.

Mara grabs my hand, clutching it.

"I am keeping something from Kaden. I mean, he deserves to know, but I don't know how to tell him."

"You can tell me," I continue, hoping she will not notice that we are standing in the middle of the street.

"Well," she whispers. "I'm pregnant."

Chapter Twenty-Nine

The word stunned doesn't even begin to cover how I feel. There is no way Mara is lying. I can see conflict in her eyes, as she wrestles with the idea of telling Kaden about their baby.

"Congratulations…" I say warily.

"I know it's stupid to be scared to tell my own mate, but I just don't want to disappoint him," she admits.

I stare at her as she wipes away the tears from her eyes, and I can't help feeling guilty. Am I seriously about to hand over a pregnant woman to a man who might potentially start a war within every Pack?

Mara coughs and it is not a sound that insinuates sickness. It is more like out of shock or surprise, as if something possibly painful has just happened.

I know the culprit. Even before she reaches for her shoulder and pulls something from it. She is squeezing a thin, empty syringe in her hand.

"What the…" She mutters before falling face-first into my arms, but not after her eyes roll to the back of her head.

I don't have to look very far, as my eyes meet the ones of the Independence Pack Huntsman.

"Cal? What the hell are you doing here?" I question angrily.

"Ensuring you are actually going to go along with this," he comments, scaling the white picket fence of someone's property.

I roll my eyes, wishing Mara wasn't as heavy as she is. "What did you use on her?"

Cal holds up a strange device to the Sun. "Something I use on the criminals while hunting in my own Pack. A very fast-acting drug that induces unconsciousness."

He pushes strands of hair away from Mara's face. He makes a soft sound in this throat. "Sorry it had to come to this, Luna."

Even though Mara is neither Cal nor my Luna, we know that there are consequences to face when messing with the Pack hierarchy. The moment I am marked, I will join her on the same scale as an equal to our Alphas, but her pregnancy weighs heavily on me.

"You know about her condition?" I ask, as Cal takes a step back from Mara, tucking his hands behind his back.

He nods. "I shot her because I know you wouldn't have had the heart to get her yourself."

He is right. I can tell by the maturity and experience etched onto his face. Something like this is probably what he is used to doing on a daily basis.

"I parked the car down there," Cal says, pointing down the road a few feet. "We should get her there before anyone notices."

Cal takes Mara's limp body into his arms, picking her up as if she weighs nothing. It takes me a few seconds to decide whether I should follow.

As I get into the car, I hear a sound that makes every sense of hope diminish. It was what I had spent this entire mission avoiding. A shout from Kaden.

I cast a glance over my shoulder, as I see the Alpha of Vengeance standing outside Mara's house. His gaze follows Cal, who places Mara inside the car without even noticing Kaden. Then, something in him changes. Wrath is the only word to describe the expression that casts across his face.

Cal looks back for me, wondering why I haven't made it to the car yet. Then, he sees Kaden. I don't even get a chance to make it within feet of the car before it starts without me.

As the car starts down the street, I am not able to move. Maybe it is the shock of being in the presence of the Alpha of Vengeance, or maybe it is because Cal is living up to his job as a Huntsman. Mission first.

I watch as Kaden runs after the car in desperation. I'm surprised that he doesn't shift into his wolf to pursue the car. Maybe he knows it isn't worth it, or maybe he knows that a key piece of information has been left behind.

Me.

As he comes to a stop, he turns towards me and his eyes meet mine.

"Please, don't kill me."

At first, I don't think he hears me, but as his mouth curves into a roguish smile, I know my words have resounded loud and clear.

"Death is too easy, Lexia," he imparts, the tone in his voice a deadly kind of teasing.

There is no way I am getting out of this. I can see now that my only chance of survival is bartering with him.

"I promise, I can explain!"

My hands come up at his proximity, as if maybe I could push his chest and he would go flying off down the street. Instead, he just grabs my wrists, pulling me closer. I wince, feeling his hand grab the back of my neck.

I know instantly what his plans are, as his fingers find the spot on my neck, despite my protests. I know it is over, as unconsciousness shrouds my vision, and I feel exactly like Mara had only minutes before.

Chapter Thirty

I am not sure what noise I make when I surface back to consciousness, but it is hardly something that could be considered normal.

I blink and try to bring my hands to touch my face, but my wrists are bound behind the chair I am sitting on. *Everything* aches, but nothing aches more than the idea of being kidnapped by the Alpha of Vengeance himself.

"I haven't had someone visit this room for a while now," a voice says from directly behind me, just as they slap their hands down on my shoulders.

"No one has dared to cross me," says Kaden.

"Look," I start, glad that the unconscious haze is starting to fade. "You have the wrong person..."

He laughs from behind, before slowly circling me. He stops in front of me, squatting down so we are at eye level.

"Tell me what you did with Mara."

I want to tell him the truth, but I can't find the right words. Partially, it is because I don't know what Cyprian plans to do with Mara, but that answer may get me killed.

"I honestly don't know!"

Kaden narrows his eyes, not looking as if he believes me for a second.

"You know I love a good game, Lexia," he purrs. "And I am not afraid to play one in order for you to tell me where my mate is."

This isn't the first time I have heard of Kaden's strange punishments. People used to come back to me when I was living in the Vengeance Pack with wild proclamations about how cruel he was. How he messed with their minds so much, they questioned what was real.

"Please... All I know..."

"Save it," he cuts in. I watch him, as he swiftly stands again, tucking his hands behind his back. "You aren't letting me have my fun.

"I think I know the perfect way to solve this," he muses. He stoops down, dragging a finger down my chin. I clench my jaw, feeling so many emotions toward him that I am struggling to fathom.

I keep my head down, as Kaden continues to circle me.

"I feel a riddle is a good indicator of how someone thinks," Kaden proclaims as he touches my hair, teasing me.

He wanders away for a second, toward a door where a man stands. He looks mildly familiar, and I think I notice him as Kaden's brother, Kace. He hands a pair of leather gloves to Kaden.

"I wore these with Mara, so she wouldn't find out I was her mate," Kaden tells me, as he slides the gloves onto his hands. "Now, I think they are quite a tool to utilize."

His words make me cringe. *What is he planning to do to me?*

"Now, for the riddle," Kaden announces. I decide to keep my gaze on him, trying not to let him see how much he intimidates me. I know his record when dealing with criminals.

He taps his chin thoughtfully.

"If you get it right, I won't hurt you," he barters. "If you get it wrong, I will hurt you."

"Rather than your foolish games, what if I just tell you where Mara is?"

The smile that graces his face, and the way he shakes his head, gives me the answer I expect.

There is no way I am going to get out of this...

He walks behind me, and I feel the tips of his gloved fingers against my temple. I listen closely to the beginning of his riddle.

"What she can see," he starts, the pressure of his fingers increasing. It is an unfamiliar feeling of discomfort, but things become stranger as he tugs on the tight rope that binds me.

"Is to be free."

Kaden pauses for a second. "And although she thinks she can escape... I'm afraid she can't compensate...

"For the crime she committed against his mate," Kaden continues, circling back around so I can see his cold eyes. "May just have been her biggest mistake."

"And she thinks he doesn't know about the man, or the stupidity of his plan," Kaden says, his exact words making my heart jump.

The Alpha smiles knowingly, and I am forced to swallow the lump in my throat.

"And while she thinks of repaying this loan," he tells me softly. "She is not aware her thoughts are not her own."

My mind widens as I process the entire riddle, coming to one conclusion. I thought only one man had the ability...

"You can read my mind," I breathe.

Kaden smiles, clapping his hands together. I don't want to believe it. No wonder this man is so cunning, so smart and thoughtful about every move he makes.

"I knew you were smart," he comments, but I can't take anything he is says seriously.

"Who else knows?" I question.

A look of guilt streaks across his face for a moment. He never told Mara. He can scour through someone's personal thoughts and make anything he wants out of them. Yet, he kept it from his mate.

"I didn't want Mara to be any different around me," Kaden says. "I felt like it would change everything."

"Are you a Phantom?" I question, wary that he might be a stalker of the night as Grayson is.

"Not completely. When Grayson was cursed, I believe I took some of the side effects."

My mind is still trying to make sense of all the information that has just been forced upon me.

137

"So, you know I am innocent then?" I question.

He sighs deeply. "You chose to sacrifice my mate to Cyprian, a man of pure evil," he says slowly, tugging off his gloves. "And I know you don't know exactly where she is being kept."

Cyprian could have taken her anywhere by now, and I believe his magic is something none of us want to mess with.

I am about to plead to Kaden for an escape, but he cuts me off. "I know about the necklace. I know Cyprian uses it to control you."

"Is that why I am tied up? Because you think he is going to summon me out of here?"

As logical as it may be, that doesn't make it any easier to accept.

"I can't let him take the only source of evidence I have against him," he tells me.

As much as Kaden doesn't want to admit it, I can see the absence of Mara is taking a toll on him. It is obvious by the way his eyes are shadowed, and he looks perpetually tense.

Almost as if he was done with the conversation, the Alpha stalks over to his brother. He hands his gloves to him while whispering something into his ear.

"These ropes really are starting to hurt around my wrists…"

He tilts his head at me as if suspicious. "I really don't appreciate secrets."

At first, I do not know what he is referring to, but then I'm overcome by the conversation I had earlier with Mara. It is as if he is pulling strands of memory from my skull, one by one. Flashes of Mara running into the street, teary-eyed and scared. Her breathless voice trembling with uncertainty. Before I know it, her secret escapes from my lips…

"She's pregnant…"

After the words spew from my mouth, I sit in shock. My body is drained from his power. He pauses for a second, letting the information sink in. All I can do is watch as he takes in the daunting news.

Oh Mara… I am sorry.

"Mara… is pregnant…" His words are drawn out and slow.

138

I can see emotion dancing in his eyes. I see glimpses of happiness, surprise, sorrow, and anger. Anger is what encompasses his being. Not anger towards Mara, but towards Cyprian. His mate is vulnerable, and he knows the harm Cyprian can cause.

Chapter Thirty-One

It takes an hour before Kaden is able to compose himself.

During his frantic state, he lets me out of my bonds and moves me from the dungeon into his office. He says the dungeon is too confining for him to think in. Even though we move, he does not trust me, nor Cyprian. Therefore, he ties me to a chair, once again.

"So, when did this ability come on?" I ask Kaden as he paces behind his desk, fingers tapping his chin as he carefully thinks.

"After Mara and I were fully mated. It was almost like it triggered it."

He is trying to figure out how he is going to get Mara back, which first means finding out where she is being kept. Kaden mentions knowing of the house I had been summoned to that night, but we both decide that Mara being kept there isn't in the realm of possibility.

"But I can't read everyone's mind. Typically, other males' minds are blurry. Even ones like yours and Mara are sometimes unreadable," Kaden tells me.

I remember Jasper telling me something about how his powers took many years to perfect.

"So, you can't really read Mara's mind then? Is that why you didn't know she was pregnant?" I ask.

"Even when I can, I can't bring myself to do it," he admits.

I twist my wrists in my ties, which Kaden has replaced with a satin ribbon after the ropes started to leave marks. Now, I am less of a prisoner and more of a liability.

"You need to tell Grayson I am here. I am sure he is freaking out right now," I tell Kaden, to which he responds with a nod. After the events of the past two days, he is well aware of what it feels like to lose a mate.

Kaden is too stressed to construct some cruel, diabolical plan to get Mara back, which also most likely involves killing Cyprian. However, Kaden never attempts to ask me for advice during his bout of concentration. Maybe, his anger is preventing him from asking for my help. It could also be his sense of pride. The pitfall of all Alphas.

***

Kaden finds a spare room for me within his estate. I am just thankful that it is not another torture room.

Reluctantly, I agree to having my arm tied to the bedpost for the night, which I suppose helps me further understand what Grayson deals with every night, minus the silver chains.

In return, Kaden agrees to call Grayson and summon him over as soon as he can.

Sleep only graces me for a few moments before I am suddenly awoken, but it isn't because of a sound. It's like an insistent tugging on the lines of my dreams, willing me to become conscious.

I try sit up properly, but the ribbon around my wrist stops me short.

The window to the bedroom is wide open; the slight breeze is cool against my skin, caressing the skin exposed from the nightclothes Kaden has let me borrow. The moonlight shines through a window, exposing something that has my heart stop completely.

A man sits on the ledge of the window, leaning against the side as his feet dangle casually. I can see the strangest color of blue tint in his hair.

"Who are you?" I whisper, my voice still thick with sleep.

The man chuckles, a sound almost musical, foreign.

"Naturally, it is the work of Fate, and good is always the work of art."

For some reason, I don't question his nonsense. The man hops from the window, and into the room. I still can't see his face, shadows concealing his identity from me.

"I am not used to travelling through the night, or visiting Alpha's mates, unbeknownst to them," he says. I can see he is holding something, but what it is, I am unsure.

He wanders a little closer. "I know that this isn't quite the reception I was hoping for, but may I say that it is my honor to meet you. You may call me Fate."

My only knowledge of Fate is that many people don't believe in him because most people only believe in the Moon Goddess.

"Interesting name."

"Isn't it?" he chuckles, gliding around the room. The moonlight gives me brief glances of his sharp, unfamiliar features. "But it isn't my name you should be so fascinated by. It is what I am capable of doing, and one of those things is gracing you with your very dear mate, the Alpha of Freedom."

I don't remember learning about Fate too much in my Pack, but I did learn to sense the honesty in someone's words. I can tell this man is not like me. He is not a normal Werewolf. He is a creature of destiny.

"What do you want with me?"

As he turns for a brief second toward the window, I catch a glimpse of his teeth flashing in the moonlight. "Grayson visited me," he replies.

"Why?"

"He wants me to do a favor for him. He wants me to kill Cyprian, who I must admit, I have never liked very much," Fate says, as he comes to a stop at the foot of my bed.

"I didn't tell him I would do it. Yes, I want him to die, but I would rather see him suffer. I know who can grant me that pleasure."

All of a sudden, the lights in the room flicker, making me cringe and close my eyes.

When I open them, I see Fate, in all his strangeness, with a knife in his hands. This isn't any old kitchen knife. The blade is long and almost paper-thin, with carvings of soft, swirling black patterns I cannot decipher.

"You have the power to change everyone's fate, including mine. If you use this knife, made specially to remove the soul from any otherworld entity, then every issue you are dealing with will diminish," Fate murmurs.

I have to swallow to stop myself from crying out. "And who do you expect me to kill?"

"The Moon Goddess," Fate explains, admiring the blade of the intimidating knife in his hand. "She and I have a history not worth retelling, but I can tell you that her death will benefit us both greatly."

I start tugging on the ribbon around my wrist.

"If you do not choose to accept the honor of using this knife to end all conflict in the Pack Quarter, then I can assure you that fate will become you biggest nightmare, and I don't mean me."

I shake my head. "I can't... I won't."

All of a sudden, a shrill scream sounds from downstairs, carrying all the way up to the room. Fate raises an eyebrow.

"Fate works in mysterious ways, Lexia," Fate says, before vanishing right in front of me.

I wrestle with my bonds for a few moments before I'm finally free. The screaming is persistent, and only gets louder as I stumble downstairs.

I bump into Kaden before I can make it to where the scream originates from. I am half-naked with mussy hair, and my eyes slightly cringe from the bright lights.

We make it to the kitchen, not uttering a single word to one another. I almost fall to the floor at what I see.

Mara is standing directly in the middle of the kitchen, tears streaming down her face as she sobs uncontrollably. On instinct, Kaden goes to move toward his mate, but I slam my hand out against his chest to stop him from moving any further.

There is a pleading look in her eyes as she holds up a blade against her neck.

Chapter Thirty-Two

I slowly hold my hands up, trying not to look at the knife that is inches away from ending Mara's life.

I can tell it takes every ounce of Kaden's being not to grab for Mara. Our proximity allows me to feel the way his hands quiver, fighting the urge to react.

"Tell us what is happening," I say calmly.

Mara looks terrified as her muscles tense, trying to fight the blade from slicing her throat. Some unknown force is obviously controlling her.

"He is controlling me! He's going to kill me!" She says, her voice rising to borderline hysteria.

Kaden and I exchange glances, immediately knowing to whom she is referring.

Cyprian.

"What does he want?" I ask warily as I go to take a subtle step closer, but Kaden catches my arm.

The look on his face is something that will forever be imprinted onto my mind. Grief-stricken, distressed, and pained. Everything he is feeling emulates perfectly what any mate would feel in a situation of utter hopelessness.

"Kaden," she whispers. "He wants Kaden."

My blood runs cold. Of course he wants Kaden. Kaden is the only one in this room that can't be controlled by Cyprian. In addition, Kaden being taken is a much bigger risk than Mara, or myself, since he is the Alpha of one of the most notorious Packs in the Quarter.

Was this his plan all along?

"Can you put the knife down?" I ask her, trying to keep my voice from shaking.

In response, the knife in Mara's hand gets unnervingly close to her neck, the tip of the blade presses against her skin. A drop of blood drips down her neck and onto her blouse.

"We have to do something!" I insist to Kaden, watching how the blade threatens Mara's life with every second.

Kaden doesn't look convinced. Cyprian could take over the Vengeance Pack by making Kaden start a war. However, this is his mate…

He signifies his defeat by falling to his knees. The knife instantly falls from Mara's hand, clattering down onto the kitchen floor. That is when I feel the tug of my entire being move in one direction. Cyprian has regained control of me, and I have an idea what is about to happen next.

Kaden is on his feet again, moving toward his mate. However, the moment he reaches out for her, she vanishes, disappearing into thin air.

We both stand their stunned.

"That son of a bitch!" Kaden snaps, raking his hands back through his mussed hair. "Cyprian is going to kill her!"

I want to respond, but my body is paralyzed. Cyprian has his fingers curled around my soul, and now he is summoning me toward him with a spell I have no choice but to obey.

"He is taking me!" I scream, my feet taking shaky steps toward the kitchen door. My hands quiver, as I try to fight against Cyprian's power.

Kaden grabs my arm, but instantly he flinches away, as if he has been shocked. We both realize there is nothing we can do.

"Follow me," I tell him, accepting the relentless pull, allowing my legs to walk out of Kaden's house.

Kaden helps me into his car, and the spell allows him to drive us with my direction. We sit in silence as hours pass. Both of us are too anxious to speak.

What we are going to encounter when we make it to Cyprian's, is unknown. That is the frightening part. What if we walk in there, and we are killed almost straight away?

"Calm down," Kaden murmurs softly. "Everything will be okay. I will get us out of this."

His words aren't convincing because I know he is worried. At this moment, all I can think about is Grayson. He would know what to do and how to calm my nerves. He would say exactly what I would want to hear, but as we get closer to our destination, I know I will never see him again...

***

As we pull into Cyprian's Pack, and park the car in front of his home, I feel a force pulling me once again. Kaden follows me, a look of confidence written across his face. It may be a façade, but he isn't about to let anyone to know this is getting to him.

Once an Alpha, always an Alpha.

Each step into the house is filled with impending dread. This could be the end.

Cyprian stands in the middle of the room, smiling at me with a triumphant grin. However, his grin is not what takes me off guard. What paralyzes me are the people I see standing in front of him.

Grayson, Jasper, and Mara are on the ground, kneeling, with their hands tied behind their backs. The moment I meet my mate's gaze, I can see the obvious pain. I want to fall to my knees and grab him. I want to be the one to free him, but he shakes his head at me, his silver eyes glinting with faint tears.

"Glad you finally made it," Cyprian says, clapping his hands together, which makes Mara flinch. She isn't looking up, not even at Kaden. Her hair is covering her face.

"And you brought company," he adds, motioning to Kaden, whose jaw clenches in response. "How convenient."

Despite wanting to challenge Cyprian's gaze, I find myself continuing to glance at Grayson.

146

"Let Mara go. You wanted me, not her!" Kaden immediately begins to barter.

My gaze wanders to where Cal stands by the door. Once, he had saved me, proving to me that he truly is a good man. Above anything, he is loyal, and I know that what he has done has been for his Pack.

"I don't think so," Cyprian murmurs, strolling over to Mara. She doesn't move, as he begins to stroke her hair. "I think I like having her here."

The moment those words come out of Cyprian's mouth, Kaden growls threateningly, looking as if he is about to shift and attack him. Somehow, he manages to keep himself from lashing out.

"Now, would you like to hear my master plan?" Cyprian asks, raising an eyebrow at me. At that moment, I am forced to my knees, right in front of Jasper. He keeps his gaze towards the ground, his expression one of defeat.

Kaden remains standing as Cyprian chuckles at the Alpha's audacity.

"Get on your knees, *Alpha,* or I will show your mate exactly how serious I am about this."

Closing my eyes, I pray Kaden doesn't do anything stupid in this situation. Thankfully, I notice the way Mara silently raises her head, and her eyes meet Kaden's. Her eyes beg him to shove his pride away. He does so, falling to his knees beside me.

Cyprian claps his hands again. "Well, this has gone much better than I expected. Now that I seem to have all your attention, I would like to explain what is going to happen from this point on. Please note that if one of you steps out of line, you will be punished."

Grayson catches my gaze at that moment, a look of pain flashing across his eyes. I want to reach out to him, but who knows what will happen if I try.

"There is another Alpha I need at my mercy, and I have an idea of how I can bring him around. The males will not be pleased to hear this, but I need a beautiful female to take this on."

The moment he says this, Mara looks up in fright. However, I am surprised when he stoops down in front of me. "I think you will do."

If Grayson wasn't tied down, I am sure that he would have done something. Instead, he just watches, his eyes are soft, and his muscles are tense.

"What do you want?" I snap, wishing I could bite his hand as he brings it up to my face, gripping my chin so I have to look him in the eye.

He smiles softly. "Alpha Malik will have fun with you."

"No," I growl instantly, the blue-eyed player flickering into my mind. "He wouldn't."

Cyprian chuckles, as if he is enjoying my retaliation. "I want you to infiltrate his Pack, and if all goes well, make it into his bedroom, where you will drug him," Cyprian tells me, fingers tightening on my chin.

I shake my head, his hands dropping from my chin.

"You're an…"

"Don't think getting angry at me will get you out of this," he mutters. "Once I have his Pack captured, the war can truly begin."

Chapter Thirty-Three

Admittedly, the Love Pack is beautiful.

Cal is driving towards Malik's estate, as I stare vacantly out the window. Glistening snow dresses everything, from the houses and gardens, to the spindly trees by the roadside.

Apparently, this Pack is always cold, but everyone seems to be perpetually merry.

My mission is simple: I present some story about Grayson and I having a fight, or something along those lines, and hope that Malik will be stupid enough to fall for it. This is our only option, unless I kill the Moon Goddess, but who knows what that would do.

Cal catches my gaze in the rear-view mirror. "Everything is going to be okay, you know that, right?"

I don't answer.

Malik's place is bigger than his ego, and that is saying something. It is hidden within a snow-laden forest, concealed from anyone who might enter without permission.

Cal parks directly in front of the house, with no security in sight to question us.

"Good luck... Remember, you're keeping many people alive," Cal tries to reassure me as I open the car door.

The air around me is brisk. *How can these Love Pack members deal with this?*

Cal drives off and I clamber up the snow-laden stairs, to Malik's main door. Knocking on the door, I wait, rubbing my hands up and down my arms in an attempt to warm them. For a long moment, no one answers, until finally I hear footsteps coming toward the door, and the sound of soft whistling.

Then none other than himself, Alpha Malik of Love, opens the door.

"Lexia?" he says in disbelief.

Without even explaining my presence, I push past him, glad for the envelopment of heat that consumes me. Malik closes the door behind me, looking at me with absolute confusion.

"Malik," I say meekly, rubbing my hands together.

The Alpha looks like he always does. For whatever reason, he favors the color black in his clothing selection, which I think anyone can admit, suits him. It makes those glacier-blue eyes stand out.

"Can I ask what you're doing here?"

This is where the lies come into play. I hate the deceit, especially as I look at the Alpha that I am supposed to seduce, but if I don't do this, then people will die. I bite the inside of my cheek.

"I need to talk to you. It's about Grayson and me."

Instantly, his expression goes from confused to worrying. Him and Grayson are both very young, and tend to get on very well. Perhaps Malik thinks something is wrong with Grayson's health, or something worse...

After making me a hot drink and offering me a seat in his living room, I finally have the chance to explain myself, with the straightest face I can possibly muster.

"I thought it would be best if I came to the Alpha of Love for this," I say, feigning some sort of innocence.

In less than a second, Malik understands what I am implying.

"You're having problems, aren't you?" he murmurs.

My heart skips a beat, as I imagine him referring not to our love life, but to our current situation. He sits in front of me, looking more mature than I have ever seen him. It suits him well, as he stares intently into my eyes.

"We had an argument. I don't think I can be with him anymore," I tell him, even sighing at the end for extra effect.

The words that are coming out of my mouth hurt me deeply. Never would I say this about Grayson. I love him more than anything, but Malik can't suspect this.

"I think I am going to leave him," I add quickly.

"What?" Malik says in disbelief. "You can't! He's your mate!"

"We aren't right for each other," I tell him, dejected. "He is an Alpha of Freedom, and I am from the Discipline Pack. It was never meant to work."

Malik sighs deeply, running a hand down his face.

"I understand," he murmurs, taking me by surprise, although I don't show it. "Just give yourself some time to truly think about it."

Obviously, this is the last thing I had expected, and it even makes me a little nervous as I realize this plan is going so perfectly.

I take a sip of the tea he has given me. "Will you let me stay here for a while? I have nowhere else to go."

Malik offers me a room to sleep in, and thankfully, he doesn't question the fact that I came with no clothes.

"Is there anything else you need?" Malik asks, leaning against the doorway while I stand by the double bed near the middle of the room, smoothing the bedspread out with my hand awkwardly. Turning around, I force a smile onto my face. It's not just any smile. It is one I would imagine being somewhat suggestive.

"As a matter of fact, there *is* something you can help me with."

I saunter closer to Malik, who looks at me uneasily. As I rest my hands on his shoulders, I realize I have never felt more awkward in my life. Even Malik seems to be sharing my pain, but it is obvious he is trying not to flinch away.

"I know you are used to having girls occupy your bed often," I say, forcing something like a sultry tone into my voice.

"I guess…"

I pull him into the room, closing the door behind me with my foot. It slams loudly, making us both jump, but I can't let that ruin the mood. Not that there really is one, but if I don't fight to find something there, everything will be ruined.

"Well, maybe you could consider me to be one of them," I say, wondering how I'm not cringing right now at my attempt to seduce the Alpha of Love. Maybe Alpha Asher of Desire needs to give me a few pointers.

Malik narrows his eyes at me, and at that moment, I am sure I am going to be caught. That is until he grabs me and pushes me against the wall.

Staring into his eyes, I hope I don't look terrified.

All these emotions hit, as he leans in, his warm breath fanning against my neck. Naturally, I tense, my body rejecting the idea of any male other than Grayson. Then, he leans in, his lips about to touch mine.

Until he laughs.

I stare at him, as he steps backward, laughing as if he is enjoying a personal joke. He grins at me and says, "You don't think I know you're up to something?"

I throw myself at the bed. "Oh thank the Moon Goddess for that."

Malik is still laughing when he sits down on the bed beside me. "Want to explain what just happened?"

"Not really, if I am being honest."

All I know is that my plan completely failed, and for some reason, I am grateful for that. As I finally look Malik in the eyes, I find myself wondering whether I should tell him about Cyprian. Everything has gone downhill, and it doesn't look like there is any other option.

"I was supposed to seduce you, so you would unknowingly drink something I had drugged," I admit sheepishly. This makes Malik's smile fade, finally.

Before he can question me, or kick me out of his house, I cut him off. "Cyprian."

He sighs as dread pools into his eyes. I'm not sure if it is to do with him being the Love Pack Alpha, but he is very open with his emotions.

"He has complete control over me, deciding when he needs me. If he got a personal item of yours, he would be able to control you too," I inform him.

Malik hates Cyprian as much as I do, and this news is disturbing to him.

"So, what happens if your plan fails?"

"I probably have a day before he summons me back to him, expecting you to be at his mercy," I admit.

Malik runs his hands through his hair in obvious frustration. Of course, he is not going to willingly hand himself over to Cyprian. Never in a million years.

I notice something on the dresser, and the sight of it makes me stand instantly. It gleams a dangerous silver as I approach it.

"What is it?" Malik asks from behind me.

I grab the handle, holding it up to the light. Fate's knife.

Chapter Thirty-Four

Grayson

My fists are clenched under the table, as every ounce of my anger threatens to expose itself in the form that will leave Cyprian with a black eye.

"Alphas have always fascinated me," he muses, dragging those infuriating fingers across my ring, the one thing that will keep me from turning into a Phantom Wolf when the Moon rises, and the Sun falls. He is using it to control me, forcing me to sit here and patiently listen to him.

He holds the ring up to the light. "Something about them makes me so... Angry."

"You don't have to do this," I whisper. "Start a war."

Cyprian laughs, tossing my ring up into the air and catching it.

"I have to start this war, Mr. Freedom. The people want war!"

I narrow my eyes at him. "The people don't want this. They want..."

Cyprian growls, cutting me off. "Don't act like you know what they want!" He snaps, leaning forward across the table.

"You failed The Test, didn't you," I murmur.

You'd have to be blind not to see Cyprian is from the Wisdom Pack. Those blue eyes and dark hair. However, to be in that Pack, you have to *belong*. To do that, you have to be exceptionally smart. They figure out your worth through 'The Test'. The Wisdom Pack is one of the only Packs which chooses who comes into the Pack.

It tests your ability to fathom, to perceive, and retain information. You need to be intelligent to the core, mentally fit.

"That test was foolish, rigged," he mutters.

Rigged? What a convenient excuse.

The Wisdom Pack's Alpha, Alden, is a good man. His Pack may have strict rules, but that is why it is one of the best. Without his Pack, half of the technology we have today would never have been invented.

"Listen, all I ask is for my ring back."

If I don't get it back by the time the Moon rises, then I will be in serious trouble. Jasper is currently in a dungeon laced with silver, ceasing his ability to use his magic.

Perhaps the beast within me could get us all out of here, but I have no doubt Cyprian is keeping my silver ring away from me for his own gain.

"Oh, you're no fun," he chuckles. "Kaden would be willing to strike a deal with me."

Kaden and Mara were placed in separate rooms. Perhaps it was because Cyprian was worried about them conspiring, or maybe he enjoys having two mates completely away from each other.

"What do you want? You have my pack ceased, and Lexia is already doing your bidding. Besides that, everything I have is useless to you," I snap, narrowing my eyes at him. He grins as he stands.

"Well, there is *one* thing," he imparts, strolling closer to me. My jaw clenches as I prepare for whatever he may force me to give up. Whatever it may be, I will not be giving it up without a fight.

He leans over the table, only inches away from me. "Your mate is very beautiful, isn't she? I love that fiery personality…"

I growl, wishing my muscles were in my full control.

He claps his hands as he walks around me. He loves to do that, in a pathetic way, to intimidate me.

"Just think of it like this, Alpha. Lexia is spending her time with neither of us right now. Instead, she is seducing none other than the Alpha of Love, and I am sure it is going very well…"

***

Lexia

"It does what?" Malik asks, as I am holding Fate's knife in my hands.

"It steals the soul from any entity, no matter how powerful they may be."

Malik's face twists uneasily, and he is obviously not sure why I have it with me. I run my finger down the blade as Malik asks, "And why may this be relevant to our current situation?"

Shaking my head at him, I steal the knife away from his gaze, hiding it behind my back. Deciding whether to share my plan with him is difficult. As the Alpha of Love, the mission could be a tough one for him to fathom.

"I have to kill the Moon Goddess," I tell him.

He hesitates, letting the words sink in. For a moment, I see nothing that would suggest any kind of reaction. Instead, those iconic blue eyes just stare blankly at me.

"You really aren't yourself, are you?"

"You need to believe me," I insist, holding the knife up again, which makes Malik flinch. "If I do this, then Cyprian will no longer have his magic to control us. We will be free, and no war will start."

Malik shakes his head, confirming what I already know to be true. He doubts how I could possibly get close enough to the Moon Goddess. How I would even have the ability to see her, let alone stab a knife into her heart.

First, I explain to him how Cyprian uses the Independence Pack's former Alpha to communicate with her, bringing her close enough to earth so he can manipulate her. That is where I will come in, and finally end this.

"That's funny," Malik says, after hearing my explanation.

"What is?"

"The fact that you don't consider what will happen to the world if you actually do kill her. She controls mates, she controls…"

"No," I cut him off. "I told you she has no real power, except from the prayers she receives."

Obviously, this isn't getting through to him. His entire Pack is almost like the Purity Pack. They worship the Moon Goddess, seeing everything she does as a blessing. Mates is something I have learned not to take for granted.

"Without her, you and Grayson may not have ever met," he tries to explain to me, except I only roll my eyes.

"Are you not the one who said you will never find a mate?" I question.

Malik knows that everyone is aware of his relationships with many women. I really do hope that whoever his mate is, she doesn't hate him for what he has done.

Malik narrows his eyes. "Don't talk about my mate."

"Trust me, please. At any moment, Cyprian is going to demand me back to him, and if I don't have you with me, either I or Grayson will be seriously hurt," I explain to him, the desperation in my voice rising with every word.

Malik is a good man who wants nothing but peace. I can see him battling within himself for a way to resolve this without disrupting too much.

Chapter Thirty-Five

Cyprian claps as we walk into the room.

"You're just in time," he notes, raising an eyebrow at both Malik and I.

Malik's presence is almost like a gift. After explaining my entire plan, the Alpha of Love had simply ridiculed me. His belief in the Moon Goddess is too strong, but the moment Cyprian began to summon me back to him, Malik hastily agreed, trying to convince me that he would get me out of this situation.

Not that I believe it for a single second.

All of my hope lies on the knife tucked into the back of my pants.

"The Sun will be setting very soon, and the moment that happens, I think we will all be graced with Grayson's *other side,*" Cyprian says.

Where Kaden is, I don't know. Mara is here, standing at the other end of this room, not tied down, but still not in control of her own body. Grayson stands opposite her on the other side of the room, with Cyprian beside him. This whole situation is a set up, and it becomes clear that something malicious is about to happen.

"I think we might all leave if that happens," Cyprian says, in a tone that can only be described as cheerful. "Well, except Mara."

My heart sinks at his words. His plan is to allow Grayson's uncontrollable beast to surface, so that he will kill Mara. Mara keeps silent, trying to be brave, but I see the lone tear trail down her cheek as she comes to terms with what her future may be. Grayson looks just as distraught, his fists clenched as he fights against the hold Cyprian has over him.

"And then, Malik, we can talk about what I have in mind," he continues, making Malik tense beside me.

"I have no interest in whatever you have to say to me. If you would like me to hand my Pack over to you, you will have to let these innocent people go."

I think everyone is surprised by his words, including Cyprian.

"You're a smart man, Malik. Unfortunately, we will have to convene over this later, as by the look of it, the Sun is beginning to set," Cyprian says smoothly, nodding to the window. He is right; the sky is stained by sunset colors of pink and orange.

I have to do something, now.

The Moon Goddess must be summoned for me to be able to stab her, but the only one who can summon her is Cyprian.

Cyprian ushers us out, and I cast one last glance at Grayson. His expression is grim; his silver eyes are filled with pain. He has no idea about the knife, nor what Fate wants me to do.

"I'll get you out," I mouth to him and Mara, although I can see their doubt from a mile away.

"I want you to send me in there instead. Sacrifice me." I say to Cyprian.

Cyprian, who has begun to walk away, pauses.

"What did you say?" Cyprian questions, as his crystal eyes glow with excitement.

I take a deep breath. "Send me in there, instead of Mara. She has nothing on you, and I do."

What I was proposing obviously appeals instantly to Cyprian. I can tell that by the way he is looking at me. This is what I want. This is what I *need.*

"You want your mate to end your life?" he asks, the question so sadistic, but he says it with a gleeful smile.

Malik nudges me again, stabbing his elbow into my side. Clearly, he is alarmed, because this is most definitely not what he discussed as a plan. Right now, I don't even have a plan. All I can think about is how I need to get Cyprian to relax his power on me, so I can actually pull the knife out to begin the original plan to kill the Moon Goddess.

"If it means Mara and her baby can survive... then yes, I will sacrifice myself," I say, trying to keep my voice from shaking.

Cyprian grins wildly. "Well, that's a game changer."

He strolls forward, standing directly in front of me to assess me.

"You know what, I think that is a great idea," Cyprian says, tilting his head slightly.

Suddenly, the power he has over me releases, and I slump in relief. The feeling of his presence leaving my body is more than satisfying, but I know he could sneak his way back in without any hesitation.

When we walk back into the room, Grayson has his hands on Mara's shoulders, looking as if he is giving her a pep talk. Her hands are over her face, and I know she is crying.

"Well, Grayson, it looks like your mate thinks she is a hero," Cyprian says, making both Grayson and Mara look up.

"What are you doing?" Grayson questions.

Cyprian grabs Mara's arm, and drags her out of the room. As she moves past me, she shakes her head at me, but I see how grateful she is.

"Good luck, mates!" Cyprian says, as he shuts the door.

It is at this moment that I realize that my plan isn't going to work. There is no way I am going to get anywhere close enough to stab her. To steal her soul. The soul that she lost when she bestowed it upon the people in a way to end the war, and start the creation of the Packs.

"Wait!" I call out, making Cyprian pause.

"What could you possibly want now?" Cyprian askes irritably.

Grayson should be turning any second now.

I know that it is something I am potentially going to regret, but if I don't do anything, Grayson is going to kill me. Then, none of them will ever have a chance to escape from Cyprian.

"Stand in front of me," I say, my voice slightly shaking. "And tell me why you want to do this."

He narrows his eyes at me.

"You owe me that much," I whisper.

He smiles slightly, tucking his hands behind his back as he strolls closer to me. I don't take my eyes off his, as my own hands reach behind me, fingertips clutching the handle of the knife.

"Luckily for you, you won't have to deal with ever being an outcast from your own Pack," he tells me.

For a moment, before I pull the knife out, I feel a flicker of sadness for him. Not being a part of your own Pack must be hard to deal with. It turned him into who he is today, wanting revenge against the Pack system. Once, I had felt the same way.

The difference is that I had the chance to get over it. He never will...

As I pull the knife out, both Grayson and Cyprian see it, but neither have time to react. I close my eyes and plunge the knife straight into Cyprian's stomach.

I don't open my eyes as I feel his warm blood against my hands. I can feel the knife's power, stealing his magic from him, sucking his soul completely out of him and taking his life with it.

"Lexia!"

The sound of my mate's voice in my ear finally makes me force my eyes open.

My hand is still wrapped around the handle of the knife, except it isn't embedded in Cyprian. He is now lying on the floor, dead. Grayson is shaking my shoulders, trying to make me awaken from my state of shock.

"You killed him," Grayson murmurs, as he pulls me against him, wrapping his arms around me. "You saved us..."

Pulling back, I look him in the eyes, wanting to do nothing than sigh with relief. Instead, I kiss him, pouring all the angst of the last few days into this intimate moment.

He immediately pulls back, and stoops down to grab his ring out of Cyprian's pocket, just in time to save himself from shifting.

We leave Cyprian's body untouched as we wander outside, to see Mara and Malik pacing the room.

"What happened?" Mara questions, watching us with complete disbelief in her eyes.

Chapter Thirty-Six

Grayson's optimism is heightened on our drive back to the Freedom Pack.

I don't blame him for being happy about Cyprian's death because I am too, but the feeling of his blood on my hands leaves me uneasy. Grayson reassures me things between the Packs will be repaired, and everything will go back to the way it was before Cyprian's influence.

Still, I'm uneasy.

The rest of the drive I fall asleep.

***

"We're home," I hear Grayson say through the haze of my slumber.

I open my eyes, seeing a pair of the softest silver ones looking back at me. Despite the obvious relief to be back in his own Pack, Grayson looks tired.

Glancing out the window, I see he is right. The trees unique to this Pack surround us, and the heat is as invading as I remember.

"Finally," I mutter, cracking the car door open.

The joy of being home is written all over Grayson's face. Being the Alpha he is, Grayson leaves me alone in the house for a while as he goes to brief his Pack on what has happened over the past few days.

I enter the house, comforted by the familiarity.

***

Grayson is back from his Alpha duties.

"Are you okay?" he asks, as I sigh deeply, closing the book I was reading.

Standing, I nod, turning around so I can see my mate. For the first time since I met him, he looks presentable. The suit he is wearing fits him nicely, and I now know that he is taking his role as Alpha very seriously.

"I'm fine," I say, wrapping my arms around his neck. His scent is comforting. "Just some things on my mind."

The concern in his eyes is evident, but his response is meant to be truthful. "Well, can I take your mind off it?"

Talking about Cyprian is the last thing I want to do right now. All I want is to be distracted, and Grayson is the only person who knows how to keep me occupied. I wrap my arms around him, and press my lips to his. Grayson picks me up, beginning to carry me away up the stairs.

The moment we are in the bedroom, Grayson sits me down on the edge of the bed. Breathless, I watch him pull off his shirt. Before he grabs me again, I take a moment to admire every dip and curve on his body.

"I've waited so long for this," he murmurs, as I pull my own shirt off.

As I lie back onto the bed, Grayson follows, looming over me. The silver in his eyes glints with excitement, showing me a side of him I haven't seen before. The feeling of his soft touch, erupting sparks across my skin has me arching my back, begging without words for more than just his touch.

My fingers run through his hair, as he gently kisses my neck, hinting at what we both want.

Running his hands down my body, Grayson slides my pants slowly down my legs. He kisses his way down between my breasts, past my stomach, and to the line of my underwear, which he takes off with any hesitation.

"I want you," I murmur.

With a soft smile, Grayson moves up my body, and I anxiously watch him tug his pants and underwear off, while I tear my bra off

164

in an attempt to hurry this along. Clearly, by the pace he is forcing me to endure, he didn't properly hear me say I wanted him.

When he leans over me, I kiss him once, which makes him smile. "Ready?"

I nod frantically, lifting my hips up to him.

As I dig my nails into Grayson's shoulders, I feel him slide into me, and I gasp. It makes me moan in relief, in pleasure, before my mate ceases my sounds by kissing me.

Instantly, I wrap my legs around his waist, as he begins to move slightly faster, each thrust having me grip his arms and throw my head back in ecstasy. Just feeling him seems to complete me, rendering me useless to anything but his touch.

He kisses me feverishly, astounding me. The sensation of him inside me, and his lips on mine, is a heady mix that I have the feeling Grayson shares.

"Oh... God," I say breathlessly, drawing my nails down his back as his hips roll against mine, giving me an immense amount of pleasure with every thrust.

I feel Grayson's teeth scraping lightly against my neck, making me moan as I anticipate what is coming next. With my head tilted back, my eyes tightly shut, I almost scream Grayson's name as I find my release in an eruption of tingles and heat, the feeling of him sealing the mark being what pushes me over the edge.

Finally, we are one.

Grayson follows soon after, breathing my name after he releases my neck from his bite.

With a kiss to my forehead, Grayson rolls off me. I glance at him, still dazed by what has just happened.

"I love you," Grayson whispers, brushing hair off my face.

I only just murmur a reply, before exhaustion hits me, and I feel myself drifting into sleep, wrapped in Grayson's arms.

***

As I wake, I can't tell what time it was. Grayson is dead asleep beside me, arm draped over his head, covers barely over him. His chest is illuminated by the moonlight streaming through the window, almost forcing me to take a few moments to admire him.

When I finally look away from him, I see the reason why I have woken suddenly in the middle of the night.

Fate.

He is sitting casually, his legs crossed on the edge of our bed, as if it is the most normal thing someone should do.

"Lexia," he says smoothly.

Instantly, I scoot back in the bed, bringing my knees to my chest. "You can't just show up in someone's room without permission," I growl.

Fate chuckles, sliding off the bed. "He isn't going to wake up. Not until our conversation is over," Fate muses, beginning to pace the room. The way he does is graceful. "I am here because we have something very important to discuss."

I am tempted to wake Grayson up, but something tells me not to.

"Congratulations on killing Cyprian. I am sure you are very happy with yourself," he says, his eyes flickering with no emotion.

He chuckles. "With my knife too."

"I had to do it," I tell him insistently.

Fate shakes his head. "You didn't do what I asked. I wanted you to kill the Moon Goddess, and you crossed me," he says, his tone darkening with every word.

I need to convince him that I had no choice but to kill Cyprian, but it is clear that Fate is in no position to listen to me. The man is used to getting what he wants.

"You should have killed her, Lexia," Fate whispers. "Because you've just made a deadly enemy."

Chapter Thirty-Seven

Jasper

I stare at the book spread open in my hand. Every drawing is so intricate, matching the vivid dreams I've had for over 300 years. At first, I didn't know why I had them about her. Every night, without fail, I would see the exact same face. After a dozen times, I finally decided I needed to draw it in a book to ensure I wouldn't forget her.

One day, I hope that she sees my face. My mate.

I know who she is and that she was born into this century. Fate works in the strangest of ways. He chose when my mate was to stumble into my life. Unfortunately, now, she and I can't be together.

Angrily, I slam the book shut, shoving it back into the spot at the bottom of my bookshelf where it has been for the last few centuries. Sometimes, I think it is taunting me.

"Such an unfortunate turn of events, isn't it?"

I twist around, and to no surprise, I see Fate sitting on one of my chairs in the living room. He is the only person who could manage to sneak into my house without me noticing. He also happens to be the only one who I can't control with my magic.

"Whatever you're here for, I'm not interested," I snap.

He chuckles, his legs draped over the arm of the chair. Sometimes I wish I could read his mind, but every time I even try to venture in, the complicated maze of thoughts gives me a headache. Just his thoughts create this weave in time, and for me to even try and infiltrate it might send me into a pit of insanity.

"Don't act like you waited this long for a mate, to suddenly have that taken away," he says, raising an eyebrow at me. "Don't act like you aren't mad."

He is wrong. How could I be mad when my major downfall is now dead? Lexia did what had to be done without thinking about its effects. She stopped a war and saved hundreds of lives. I will deal with the consequences because that is an Alpha's job. Even if it means I will be without a mate for as long as I live, which will be a very long time.

"You need to leave," I growl, not moving an inch. The moment I take my eyes off him, the moment he has more free rein of my house. I'm also trying my hardest to protect the book from his prying eyes.

He stands swiftly. "I have a proposition for you. In the end, you and Thea can be together."

I knew that was what he was going to propose. Nothing in my life is worth anything compared to my mate. Now that my heart doesn't look to be beating anytime soon, a part of me sparks with interest at his words.

"What may that be?" I question, folding my arms over my chest.

I don't want him to think that he can play his ridiculous games with me. Not many people know much about how Fate works, but I do. The amount of power he has is extreme, but his ability to use it is mitigated by the Moon Goddess.

"I need one of your allied Independence Pack members. How you get along with those singing airheads is beyond me," he says, that sickening grin on his face. "However, I need one to summon the Moon Goddess. Don't worry because you won't be the one ending her life."

"You want the Alpha of Independence, I suppose," I drawl. Faye will be the hardest to convince. Her personal love for the Moon Goddess trumps everything else in her life, aside from her Pack. No one actually knows exactly where her Pack is. I use magic to transport there, but people say it is hidden deep in the mountains, sheltered from rogues and potential war.

"That would be nice, and I promise a beating heart will be your reward," he tells me.

I regard him anxiously as he walks around my living room, dangerously close to my shelves of books. Luckily, the book of drawings is tucked away from eye level, so I'm sure he will not catch a glance of it.

He stands directly in front of me. "The sooner, the better. My little knife wielder is unpredictable," he muses, raising his eyebrows.

"Why don't you just do it yourself?" I snap. "All-powerful is what you're known for, right?"

He shrugs, holding his hands up. "No use getting these dirty, when I have people to do it for me."

Casually, as if he owns the place, he strolls to the front door. "Goodbye, Alpha. I hope the next time I see you, I'll have your heart beating."

***

"Why here?" she asks, as I lay the blanket flat on the ground.

I glance up, catching the emerald gaze of Faye, the Alpha of Independence. She stares at the blanket I just placed apprehensively.

"I thought it would be a nice place," I muse, standing up again.

Fate didn't tell me exactly where he wanted the Moon Goddess summoned, however I have a feeling it won't matter. He will find me if he wants to. Therefore, I chose a place outside in the Devotion Pack, among the trees in the Phantom Forest. No one in my Pack comes here, which is perfect for concealing what is about to happen.

"You haven't told me yet why I you want me to summon the Goddess," Faye says with a worried expression on her face.

Faye's hair is as white as snow and sits along her waist. She is wearing a long dress with a corset tight to her bodice.

"You'll see," I say, aware of how cryptic my words may be. Faye sighs, and my heart sinks a little. She has trusted me for a long time. I remember visiting her family when she was just born, while listening to them preach about another female heir. Now, I am about to go against everything I stand for, as a way to not anger he who is now known as the All-Powerful.

I hand her the book I am holding in my hand. "The spells you need to summon her to earth."

She takes it, smiling gratefully. The incantation is powerful enough to not only summon her, but to keep her here long enough for Fate to do what he wants.

"Thank you, the Goddess will be forever grateful for her freedom, if you are to allow it, being the keeper of this book," Faye says, thumbing through the pages. Her accent is high and light, another way to signify her difference from the rest of the Packs.

I watch as she places the book down on the blanket she kneels on, the pages facing her are doused with italic writing in a language I am not familiar with. The book was originally from the Independence Pack, that I was granted by the Alpha herself, who was Faye's great, great grandmother, to keep safe once she died.

Faye starts singing, cutting my thoughts off. I've always known that Independence Pack members are the best singers to exist. The tune they usually sing to the Moon Goddess can even enchant a normal person. As I listen to Faye sing, I feel a little light-headed.

I don't say a word as she sings, her finger trailing under the words to keep in place. She stops very abruptly. Silence surrounds us, as Faye stands swiftly. Then she speaks. "You can come out now, Goddess."

Frowning, I look around, trying to see who she is talking to. Then, a young girl emerges from around a tree, shivering in all her bareness.

She looks so... normal. Never have I been able to say I have known someone who has lived longer than I have, but as I stare into her eyes, I realize she has. The one they pray to. The one who has suffered for many years. She is here, looking like a lost, young woman.

"You're here," Faye whispers, before running at the Goddess.

The Purity Pack would have frowned upon such informality, since they believe the Goddess is all-powerful. I watch her collapse into Faye's arms, bursting into tears. The two don't look like an Alpha and a Goddess as they fall to the ground, tears and words of glee passing between them.

"Am I free?" the Moon Goddess gasps. "Please don't send me back."

Faye pulls her to her feet, patting her hair down, wiping her tears away. The way they act suggests they are sisters, or at the very least, best friends. It dawns on me then that Faye has spent a lot of time singing to the Goddess to keep her company.

"You will have to ask Alpha Jasper," Faye says, forcing the Goddess' gaze on me.

Feeling bad doesn't even begin to cover how I feel. I have kept my end of the deal, having summoned her, but now, all I want to do is have her escape into the woods.

Before I have made a decision, Fate appears with a baffled Lexia on his arm.

Epilogue

Lexia

My first movement is to pull desperately away from Fate, ripping my arm from his grasp.

Stumbling backward, Jasper catches my shoulder protectively. For a fleeting moment, I am able to recover a little bit of my sanity. I don't know how Fate managed to get us here.

"Fate, what are you doing here?" a woman to the right of Jasper questions.

Her hair is whiter than I have ever seen, like untouched pages of a freshly printed book. Her eyes are an unexplainable green, bright and vibrant like pure emerald.

Even though her beauty is stunning, my attention is focused on a girl standing behind her.

"Oh, he didn't tell you, Faye?" Fate questions, his face lighting up as he motions to Jasper.

The name Faye sounds familiar. I believe she is the Alpha of Independence. Holy Goddess, I am in the presence of the only female Alpha.

"Tell me what?" she questions, in a singsong accent that caresses my soul.

Jasper suddenly pulls me behind him. "I did what you wanted; I want my heart to beat again. I want you to let Faye go."

Confusion is written all over Faye's face. Clearly, she is as ill-informed as I am, but at least she isn't about to kill the Moon Goddess.

"Take Faye away if you want. In fact, I suggest it. She might not want to see what is going to happen next," Fate says, casting a glance toward me.

Faye finally acknowledges me fully. Perhaps if I wasn't protected behind Jasper, she might have thought I was on Fate's side.

"And Lexia…" Jasper says, although a little more warily.

Fate laughs, blatantly ridiculing the idea of me leaving. If he was going to take me here, after breaking into my house, drugging Grayson and teleporting me with magic, then I highly doubt he would let me out of his sight for even a second.

"Go," I insist, just as Faye is opening her mouth to talk. I know she would never leave if she knew what was about to happen.

I have an idea. A potentially foolish idea, but it means Fate being completely comfortable. Something tells me Jasper's presence won't help that.

"I can't leave you here," Jasper insists, falling into the Alpha mode.

Pushing at his chest, I shake my head in protest. "If you want to be with Thea, you have to trust me."

Instantly, he pauses. This man will do anything for his mate.

"Can someone please explain…?"

Before the Alpha of Independence can say another word, Jasper grabs her arm and they disappear, leaving only the faintest sign of a shadow in their place.

The girl left behind must be the Moon Goddess. She is completely naked, shivering slightly in the cool breeze. I feel strange staring at her, as if I don't deserve to.

"Fate," she mutters. "I haven't seen you in millennia."

She sounds quite calm around him, despite the tears that have been in her eyes.

"Millicent," he murmurs. "How is the Moon?"

She doesn't answer. I just stare at my feet, unable to look at her.

"Still didn't choose you," she mutters, making my eyes widen. She speaks the same language as us impeccably.

Fate chuckles. "It didn't need to. Now, it has no choice but to choose me."

My heart sinks, as Millicent finally looks at me. She looks confused, but she also looks lost. I can see the strain of over a million years on her face. The moment we fully look at each other, she quickly looks away again.

"Not another one of your wild ideas where you think you can take my place? Fine, you know I never wanted this," Millicent says blandly, raising an eyebrow.

The fact that she is about to willingly hand her position away to the megalomaniac is a little shocking, but in a way, I understand. Being trapped by the Moon for so many years must have warranted some insanity, and I don't blame her for wanting to be as far away from it as possible.

"I can't settle for that," Fate murmurs, and my heart sinks. "You need to be dead."

As Fate hands me the knife, I notice I have her full attention. As I stare at it in my hand, the weight of the situation hits me, and I have to stop myself from throwing up.

"No," she says, her voice rising frantically as Fate grabs her arms, restricting her. "I'll go, you can take my spot. Please, don't kill me!"

The end of her sentence is directed at me, letting the feeling of dread seep deeper into the pit of my stomach.

"Please, have mercy!" At this point, she is begging, as a fresh set of tears begins to flow down her face. It kills me from the inside. There is no way I can do this.

So I turn the knife around, and face it toward my heart.

Fate doesn't even blink an eye, as a flood of emotion fills his face. He isn't worried that I am about to kill myself to save Grayson, Thea, and Jasper. He doesn't care that I clutch the handle of the blade, holding back tears as the sharpness pierces my shirt.

He just looks angry, fed up. Taking me by surprise, he snatches the knife out of my hand, making me stumble back. "I'll do it. I can't have her alive for another second…"

Pulling Millicent to him, Fate holds the knife up, and the poor girl's eyes scan it in utter dread.